Attack on the *SPORTPLATZ*

For more information:
Stephen F. Austin State University Press
P.O. Box 13007 SFA Station
Nacogdoches, Texas 75962
sfapress@sfasu.edu
www.sfasu.edu/sfapress

Book design: Shaina Hawkins
Cover design: Shaina Hawkins
Distrubted by Texas A&M Consortium
www.tamupress.com

LIBRARY OF CONGRESS CATALOGING-IN-PUBLICATION DATA
Shearer, Robert A.
Attack on the Sportplatz/ Robert A. Shearer
ISBN: 978-1-62288-118-5

This book is dedicated to

Robert L. Shearer

Contents

v

The Playing Fields of Julich

THE FIERCENESS AND DOGGEDNESS OF GERMAN resistance on the sector east of the Aachen were epitomized by their defense of a sports stadium outside the town of Julich. U.S. Ninth Army headquarters last fortnight had airily ticked it off as one of "a few pockets of resistance" remaining to be cleaned up west of the Roer River. To the dough foots of the 29th Infantry, who had to clean it up, it was quite a pocket.

Julich's sports arena was an oval enclosure formed by a mound eight or ten feet high, in which were three football fields and a concrete swimming pool. U.S. artillery and planes dealt the defenders a merciless beating. A pillbox under a haystack was unmasked and heavily shelled. But when the infantry moved in across open fields, German mines and machine guns time & again drove them back. A bridge over which the defenders for reinforcements was knocked out by the Ninth's cannon every day. Every night the Germans put it up again.

After a solid week of fighting, the 29th took the pool with bazookas, grenades, bayonets, then wiped out the last resistance at the south end of the oval. The capture had cost more U.S. casualties than the taking of many a German village. Among the U.S. wounded was a Sergeant who had had both legs blown off by a mine. To a major who came up to his stretcher, he mumbled weakly: "We took our objective sir." The major wept.

(*Time Magazine*, December 18, 1944, page 23)

Preface

THE FOLLOWING NOVEL IS A SECONDARY HISTORICAL memoir. It is historical fiction written by one person about another person's experience. This book is based on a true account of an attack by my father and the brave young men under his command on an athletic complex, *Sportplatz*, in Julich, Germany on Hitler's western wall of defense guarding the German border in the Rhineland.

War, death, pain, love, and survival are the primary themes of the book.

The goal of the book was to present the themes at the highest level of human intensity and experience: intense visceral combat; random and violent death; physical and emotional pain; deep love and commitment; and remarkable and painful survival and recovery.

The events took place during World War II near the end of the war, prior to and just after December 1st, 1944, and shortly before the Battle of the Bulge. The military personnel, locations, events, and the sequence in which they occurred are documented historical facts. The names of the soldiers involved in the battle have not been changed. The thread of subjective thoughts and conversations that provide a transition and a personalized context for the events are fictional. The personalized parts of the story are fiction for several reasons. Even though he related many of the accounts, my father never wrote them down in book form, but he did make notations in the margins of several published accounts. In addition, the official military descriptions are sketchy and incomplete. For example, the official accounts simply indicate that an attack took place on the athletic complex. Usually, no details or inaccurate details are given concerning the clash or outcome. The historical records were very valuable in corroborating the events, but they were rarely presented on a continuous personal basis. In addition, other WWII veterans, especially non-commissioned officers, typically only knew what was going on in front of them at a certain moment. They knew little of what took place before and after their arrival and departure. They also knew very little of what was taking place to their right or left of their position in battle. Nevertheless, the veterans who were consulted were very helpful because they had a remarkably keen memory after so many years had passed.

Finally, I wasn't there so part of the account draws on my research, empathy, professional education, speculative association, hindsight, and imagination to hopefully capture the futility, irony, pain, and horror of another person's experience.

Any inaccuracies, omissions, embellishments, or naiveness is my responsibility. My hope is that the account is close to an authentic and valid approximation of the original reality of the situation. The task of attempting to reach this reality was thoroughly humbling, gut-wrenching, and surreal.

There were several purposes that motivated me to write this story. The first purpose was somewhat selfish because the various fragments of the story have been in my head for too long and I wanted to put them in print. They play, sometimes dimly and sometimes loudly, like a recorded message on a randomly burned disk. So, selfishly, the first purpose is derived from some type of cathartic need to get them off my mind. The second purpose was to continue a tradition. My father was an enthusiastic and passionate storyteller. A purpose of writing this account was to continue this tradition. War stories told by some veterans after WWII were probably related as frequently as they were liberally embellished. A check of the historical record would indicate that his stories, though no doubt painful to tell at times, were not embellished or fabricated. He experienced the events and subsequently related them to an always eager and attentive audience. Being the eldest child and old enough to remember, I had greater exposure to the stories told after the war, and they no doubt made a greater impression. So, with humility, I became the storyteller.

The final purpose of this account was not only to keep the story alive for Captain Shearer's descendants but also to provide them an opportunity to appreciate the struggles and sacrifices of one member of what has been identified as the "Greatest Generation." He and my mother's stress, pain, agony, and disruption in their lives merits this small bit of literary immortality.

This book started as a writing project for my family around the turn of the twentieth century. So, this is technically an extensive revision and expansion of the original printed but not published manuscript.

The revision incorporates my changes to the original manuscript, recently discovered information about the battle, personal letters sent home from the war, and relevant articles from *Yank, The Army Weekly* magazine and *Stars and Stripes* newspaper. The first magazine was published weekly by the United States military during World War II. The first issue was published June 17, 1942. The magazine was written by enlisted rank soldiers only and was made available to the soldiers, sailors, and airmen serving overseas.

Each issue was edited in New York City and then shipped for printing around the world where staff editors added local stories. The last issue was published in December 1945.

Issues included pin-up girls, cartoons, poems, news from home, and letters to the editor. It was not an accurate historical document because stories were carefully censored to not reflect negatively on the war effort or divulge critical battlefield information like troop strengths or casualties.

The second publication is an American newspaper that reports on matters affecting the members of the United States Armed Forces. It operates from inside the Department of Defense but is editorially separate from it. During World War II, the newspaper was printed in dozens of editions in several operating theaters. Some of the editions were printed very close to the front in order to get the latest information to the most troops.

In preparing to read this account, three important factors should be kept in mind. First, most of the events took place, by western standards, in very small places. Some of the locations are difficult to find on a map. The Rhineland was dotted with small farming villages that were separated by only a few miles. Second, considering the grand scope of World War II, the battle for the *Sportplatz* was not a major event. The events have only recently been documented in history books and most people, including historians, have never heard of the events. So, the battle did not have a great historical significance, unless of course you participated in the battle or one of your loved ones was wounded or died at the scene of the battle. Finally, this account is not designed to be another "can you top this?" assertion of the horror of war. Millions of soldiers and civilians suffered unimaginatively in World War II, and the history of this physical and psychological suffering has been rightfully and extensively documented. Rather, it is more of an attempt to indicate that the heroes were not only very brave, but also human, fragile, and vulnerable to random chance. For example, the chances of surviving, physically or psychologically, two assignments in the front lines, like my father did, are mathematically very slim. On the other hand, he knew fellow officers who went from the invasion to the *Sportplatz* to the end of the war without any physical wounds. It appears that probability of a soldier's survival was left to pure chance, abject fate, or divine intervention.

—RAS

Attack on the *SPORTPLATZ*

Robert A. Shearer, Ph.D.

Stephen F. Austin State University Press

Chapter One

Back to the Front

LOOKING THROUGH THE OPEN DOOR AND THE wide spaces between the boards of the Belgian boxcar, he could see thousands of stacked and scattered wooden crates littering the sides of the railroad tracks. Each box was unmistakably stenciled in black ink with the German eagle and swastika. From the occasional putrid odor, he could tell many of the crates contained rotting food. The German Army had emptied the precious cargo in their railroad cars in their haste to move German troops in retreat in the face of the quickly advancing allied forces. They needed the old freight cars for troop movement, so the critical supplies had to be abandoned along the tracks. It seemed to him like the littered mess went on forever. It was an unmistakable sign that the mighty German Army was retreating back to the German border. He was heading that direction, and everyone knew the German Army would surely stand and fight at the border. It was assumed they would present a stiff resistance to the allies trying to enter their homeland.

The boxcar he was riding in was called a "forty-and-eight," supposedly because it was designed to hold forty men and eight horses.

These damn things obviously weren't designed to carry people.

He had never seen any horses in one, but this one had more than forty GIs in it, and it smelled like livestock had been in it. They couldn't all sit on the floor at the same time, so some stood while others sat on the well-worn wooden floor or on their backpacks.

The old Belgian and French boxcars were smaller than those he had ridden in the United States, and they must not have had any springs because they rode rough enough to jar his teeth. Fortunately, the heavy wool overcoat provided some padding on his butt against the hard wooden floor. Every time the boxcar hit a bump, all of the utensils inside their mess kits rattled in unison. Some of the dates on the sides of the cars were of WWI vintage, so he knew they had traveled along these tracks many times, but not with human cargo in many years.

The boxcars were crowded, and it was cold because the wind sliced through the cracks in the sides. The near freezing wind on his face burned like the flames from exploding fuel in a vehicle hit by an enemy cannon shell. He was thankful he had the heavy olive drab (OD) wool overcoat over his field jacket. In these near freezing conditions, a soldier could die without one. He and all of the other GIs in the car wore the same issued overcoat over their field jackets, wool sweaters, and long sleeve wool shirts.

Some men had even managed to swipe a wool army blanket from somewhere to wrap around themselves for additional protection from the cold. They looked more like medieval monks except for their Garand rifles protruding vertically from their coats and blankets. It was damn cold in the moving car, but it was better than being stuck in the congestion of Paris or Brussels or marching all the way along the muddy roads. He knew he was somewhere between Brussels and Liege, Belgium. Brussels had been devastated by allied bombing and was now in a complete civic and transportation chaos. Brussels was congested with GIs and military vehicles trying to get somewhere. There were thousands like him trying to get to the front and thousands of wounded trying to get back to England. In the midst of the chaos and confusion, there were also thousands of civilians trying to avoid all of the players in the violent drama that had shifted back-and-forth across their country. It was the same scene crossing the English Channel and in the port where he landed in order to get to Brussels. The scene in the train station was complete chaos, disorder, and insanity as the crowd of uniformed soldiers surged forward to fill the boxcars until the cars couldn't accept any more soldiers. At least, this time, crossing the channel for him wasn't as rough as waiting for D-day. This time, the water in the English Channel had been resting with two to three-foot seas, not heaving and thrashing with eight to ten-foot seas.

It was starting to rain and the rain was blowing into the forty and eight and whirling around as a fine mist. Small icicles were starting to form as the freezing rain poured off the roof of the boxcar. They didn't dare close the door on the rolling relic for fear of getting trapped inside if a shell hit it, exploded, and caused the boxcar to erupt in flames. So the rain came in the door, and they moved away from the door as far as they could.

Even though the boxcar was swaying and lurching on the tracks, the ride was a lot smoother than riding in a GMC (General Motors Corporation) two–and–a–half ton truck on a deeply rutted muddy road. He tried to not think the cynical thought that it was also a lot faster than a truck to reach their destination.

Unfortunately, it meant many of the men in the forty-and-eight might die sooner. He had seen so many men die, and he knew many of the faces he was looking at would also soon die or either be wounded. He had seen, heard, and smelled the acres of mangled, burned, and mentally disturbed soldiers in the hospitals in England.

He told himself, *Don't get emotional. Not here. Not now.*

Except for a German soldier's poor aim, I wouldn't even be here! How good are my chances another time in combat?

Ever since he got out of the hospital in England, he had experienced pronounced emotional swings. The swings went from anger to depression with intermittent various levels of anxiety-buffering the two extreme emotions. His anger was a syndrome of emotions marked by intense frustration, depression, and pent-up hostility. His depression was evidence of a combination of emotions marked by dejection, helplessness, guilt, and powerlessness.

His emotional condition was a direct result of seeing so many of his men die in combat in France, particularly the young officers under his command. The heightened emotional state of aggression in combat was jerked in an opposite direction when the young men were killed. One minute they were attacking enemy together. In the next minute, they were gone. The loss of the bright young men was overwhelming, and he couldn't do anything to prevent it or fix it. All that was left was his anger and helplessness.

These experiences and their resulting effect on his emotional balance were further amplified by the extreme suffering he witnessed in the hospital. The anger, anxiety, and depression returned to compound his emotional swings. Fortunately, he spent a lot of his period of recovery with an English family, away from the human carnage of battle.

The respite helped him take his mind off of the experiences of the past, but he still had flashbacks and periods of emotional intensity. Nevertheless, particular sights, sounds, smells, and situations could set off an emotional spell.

He could feel the spell coming on. He would tear and have a frightened and panicky expression on his face. Fortunately, the time he spent with his hosts in England had diminished his unpleasant spells. But, the potential was always lurking beneath the surface. Now, he was going back into all of the madness, evil, and death of front line combat.

Will it be death, another wound, or a complete mental breakdown?

Returning to the moment, he could also see from the open door the structural carnage and devastation the war had left in the passing countryside. Villages and cities leveled and left in rubble, passed in view along the trip. There were dead animals all along the way and the stench of decay and decomposition was a constant reminder of the destruction. Bridges were parted, mangled, and destroyed. Factories in Brussels were leveled, and most of the farm buildings were empty masonry shells or piles of rubble. The blackened shells of farm buildings stood like sentinels on the Rhineland Plain pointing the direction of more death and destruction. He also saw hastily dug graves, sometime one or two and other times acres of grave markers. An attempt had been made to ensure that no allied soldiers would be buried in Germany, so Belgium and Holland had become the sepulcher hosts of the fallen soldiers buried in warrior cemeteries.

There are soooooooo many men buried along here. What a waste. These are the poor bastards that didn't make it back to the hospital.

His unit, the 116th of the 29th Division, was somewhere near Herleen, Holland, and that was where he was headed in the godforsaken boxcar. He knew about freight cars. He had "hopped" freight trains after high school during the depression. He frequently had gone to see relatives, the Hoaglands, in Ft. Garland, Colorado. They lived in the officers' quarters of the old fort. Shorty Hoaglan had "run" with Kit Carson and hunted for him. Shorty's descendants lived there. He had fond memories of the carefree, sunny summers he had spent with his distant but hospitable relatives in the high mountain valley. But now, those experiences seemed like a long distance from Belgium, a stark contrast to his present situation, and eons ago.

When he looked at the other troops in the car, he could see they were all young, untested, and green replacements. Their eyes had that excited look as they tried to absorb all of the new events. They didn't have the far away stare, deadpan expression, flat affect, and look of indifference of traumatized combat troops. They seemed to be all privates in rank and about eighteen or nineteen years old. They also were all wearing clean uniforms. He knew the uniforms wouldn't stay clean very long. He thought he must have stood out because of his age of thirty and the obvious captain's bars on his shoulder. He almost wished he wasn't wearing the silver bars, like in combat, where the officers didn't wear their rank. If an officer wore his rank in combat, German snipers could identify a command target and kill American officers. Consequently, identifying rank was removed. In addition, divisional patches were also removed by some units. He also hoped that he didn't have that blank, far away look that he had seen on the other replacement troops who had been there before and lived in a hole in the ground, under fire, for days and weeks.

"First time to the front, captain?"

He was startled by the question that was asked by a private who looked a little older than the others, maybe twenty-one years old.

"No. I went into France," he replied.

"You were in D-day?"

"Yes. I went in on D-day plus five. I was sitting on a ship in the English Channel when the invasion started."

Before he embarked for the invasion, he wrote the following letter:

June 6, 1944

My Dearest:

Remember that date. It will live a long time in history. I could tell you so much if I was allowed hon, but let me say that if Hitler could see all that was in store for him, he would quit right now Remember the noise that used to irritate us in Dallas? Well, hon it is a thousand times greater and there is not one minute during the 24 hrs that the windows don't shake from the intensity I am sending you under separate cover my application for your travel pay from Swift to Wood. It was returned to me. Now, here is what you'll have to do. Write to Rich at Wood and tell him to get two copies of the movement orders which include the "Travel Directive Necessary" and "Procurement Authority" for movement. Then ship the application with the two copies to the finance office as directed on the letterhead. You might look thru my files first and see if can find a copy or two. It will state something like this usually at the bottom of the order.

TDN-P401-31-AT-20-2 etc.

That's just an example. Rich could get them for you I'm sure. I hope you're in the house by now. I'm getting ready to leave mine soon and leave everything behind. No boxes yet or picture of you. Tell Bill I in states got his bottle. I'm saving it until I get in a tight spot up front. When the going gets rough and I feel tough then I'll think of Bill and open his bottle. Your mother can send a box a week also you know. You might try sending gin in a bottle or something. But mainly now I'm going to be interested in food. Don't forget to send that salami.

Well dear, I've got some things to do. One is eat lunch. It's pretty tough deciding what to leave and what to take. My future is quite uncertain. Regardless hon I'll always love you. You're the only woman I've ever known or want to know. My only wish is for you.

All my love,
Bob

Now, several sets of the young eyes were fixed on him and he didn't see any way of avoiding being the center of attention. He didn't say what he really wanted to say because contemplating their future was too depressing.

"We haven't seen many officers," the private said.

"Well, there's a real shortage of officers and the few around are pretty old for this kind of action."

Yea and the ones who have been in before have nerves shot to hell!

He had seen many combat officers in the hospitals in England who had to be pulled out of the front lines because of combat fatigue. Some went back in. Others were finished, *fini la guere.*

The Great Depression had preceded the war, so few young men had been in ROTC or officer's candidate school. Consequently, there were few officers available for military duty when the war began. The army was also downsized during the depression because everybody was convinced World War One was the war to end all wars. This, along with a political sentiment of isolation, led to a crisis in the military caused by a shortage of command officers.

He was the ROTC cadet commander at Coe College where he graduated and was planning a career in the military. The night before he was to take his physical, he went to a party after a dance. The next day when he took his physical he showed to have blood in his urine, so he flunked the physical. He couldn't be sure, but it was probably the gin he drank. Anyway, the result was that he was given a reserve commission so he had to get a civilian job and start working. His present predicament started when he was on the golf course in Dallas and the news came over the radio that Japan had bombed Pearl Harbor. He knew at that moment he would have to go on active duty. After three months of basic training at Fort Benning, Georgia, he was assigned to Camp Swift near Bastrop, Texas, the closest induction center.

"What's it like at the front, captain?"

"Damned quiet, you hope. You don't want to fire your rifle if you can keep from it. You have to ration your ammo, you know, so you don't run short. If you run out of ammo, your goose is cooked."

When he was in action in France, he had to return to the beach because his and other units were almost out of rifle ammunition. He saw the reason why there were shortages when he got to the beach. A storm, right after the landings took place, had destroyed the large breakwaters that had been built, so supplies were held up from being unloaded. In fact, the entire beach landing area was a tangled mass of wreckage left by the storm. He managed to load the back of a jeep and drive it back to the front lines and his men with some ammunition that simply had been sitting on the beach and not transported to the front.

"What are you doing here?"

"I'm going back to the front. I got hit at St. Lo, and I just returned from five months in the hospital in England."

Another voice asked, "Where did you get hit?"

"A German paratrooper sniper got me in the hip. I zigged when I should have zagged, and he was a really bad shot. So, I've been lying on my ass in a hospital."

"You mean if you get wounded, you don't go home?"

"Not if you're an officer and it's classified as a flesh wound. I didn't have enough points I guess."

He reached into his pocket to make sure he still had his billfold. He wanted to make sure he had it because it contained two pictures of Skip. She sent the first picture to him when he was fighting in France back in July. It was a pin-up picture.

After he received it, he wrote the following letter to her on the 10th of July.

July 10, 1944
France

My Dearest:
Whew! That picture! My god it took my breath away. You sure caught me by surprise, Kid. I never thought I'd get anything like that. It sure is swell Kid and that is gonna be my lucky piece to carry from now on. I keep looking at it and just thinking. It really is the first time I've been shaken into feeling normal.

All my love
Bob

On July 11, 1944, he was wounded and he received the second picture while he was in the hospital in England. In the second picture, she was wearing a tailored suit she made from blue Harris Tweed cloth that he had sent her from England.

After he was wounded, he wrote the following letter:

Detachment of Patients
4129 U.S.A. Hospital Plant.
apo. 505
July 12, 1944

My Dearest Skip,

This is another of those letters I don't know how to write. All I tell you won't make any difference or you'll worry. But you don't have to hon. The simple facts are this: I was hit by a kraut paratrooper who saw me first.

He was a damned poor shot and he just grazed my right hip. I was hit about 7:30 a,m. and was in the General Hospital in England by 4:00 p.m. They evacuated me from France by air. After I was hit I crawled 200 yds. thru briars, not because I couldn't walk or run but I didn't want to give him a second chance. They got my recon Sgt. thru the shoulder at the same time. So don't worry, hon, after all, I got the Purple Heart now. That's some consolation isn't it?

Now I'm in a nice clean bed with plenty of good food. Nurses are nice and I can't even tell I've been hit. They operated on me last night and it only took fifteen minutes to do it. Now I know how it feels to have a baby. They gave me twilight sleep. It reminded of the time Ernie got me drunk.

I'm going to call Mrs. Speck tomorrow and maybe they will come to see me. I'm just about back where I was before. Better not write to this address. I want to see the doctor tomorrow to see how long I'll be here. It should be but a few weeks. In that case, you better write to a.p.o. 29. but wait till you hear from me again.

Be sure to read the first article in the July 9 YANK. It is very good and very close to home.

Well hon take good care of yourself now and don't worry. Will send you the Purple Heart when they give them out. I'm not hurt at all. In fact, it is just like the time I cut my leg making lemonade. Just about the same size cut too. Will write tomorrow.

All my love,
Bob

Skip obtained a copy of the magazine and read the first article he recommended.

North of St. Lo

The front line north of St. Lo is something very near and very indefinite like a heat mirage. It is broken up and spread out with pockets and salients of German troops up close to Allied positions.

Traveling towards St. Lo you go right on down the line from one command post to another with plenty of field hospitals, ammunition dumps, motor pools, etc. in between. None of these is technically the front line but most of them are under fire at one time or another from enemy guns and aircraft.

As we drove southward the sun mounted the sky and a very fine, clear summer evening took shape. As the jeep traveled down the hot, glaring white road it threw up clouds of dust powdering the hedgerows on either side with a light gray coating. Wherever you looked there was a steady stream of military traffic going north and south----tanks, trucks and one huge van with a KP sitting contentedly in the back surrounded by vats of coffee and great stacks of 10-in-one rations. They were on their way to supply warm meals to military police and other men on duty in remote sections. The traffic started to thin out, and finally we reached a point along the road where German mortar fire was beginning to land with some consistency. So we got out and walked the rest of the way across an open field, where the wreckage of a C-47 lay smeared all over the ground. Some of the parts had been found nearly a mile from the scene of the crash. Then on we went through bushes and thickets where a trail had been made first by driving a jeep back and forth over the brushwood, later by hacking down the shrubs with knives.

Finally, we reached a small, damp green field which was the farthermost point of the American advance. It was not very eventful looking. There were two men standing near us; one of them was leaning on his rifle, the other squatting under a tree finishing a V-Mail. Beyond the fence, a couple of cows were grazing in deep grass about a hundred yards from us. They were standing in the very spot where the night before German machine guns had been in action. Things looked very peaceful in the broad daylight, but last night, the sentry said, for two hours he had stood still at his post watching out the corner of his eye what he thought was a human figure. When the morning came, he saw it was a gate post.

We went back to the small gutted farmhouse which the officers had taken over as the company command post. There were more cows in the field around the house and a flock of chickens that yielded an average of twenty-five eggs a day.

There were about six officers and noncoms sitting around the farmhouse. Some of them were making out daily reports, others were talking about possible gun inspection by their colonel and planning a quicker method of getting fresh water down to the men every two hours if possible. There was not much for them to do right now. things were t a stalemate. they were as near the enemy as they could possibly go for the time being. (Cpl. John Preston, *Yank,* July 9, 1944)

She also obtained a later copy of the magazine and read another article about the war, where he had been, what it was like, and where he was wounded.

Battle for St. Lo

Before St. Lo---'Hedgerow warfare' is a new term, which has bludgeoned its way into the military vocabulary and will probably be taught to sweating West Point plebes for many years to come. The hedgerows in this part of the front must be seen to be believed. They are six feet high and six feet thick, and form breastworks which line every road and every field. These hedgerows were here generations before the kings of Normandy imported them to the cattle-raising sections of England, and they have been packed down into cement-like hardness by the pressure of centuries. I have seen 88mm, and 105mm shells score direct hits on hedgerows---and blast holes barely large enough for two men to squeeze through together.

Because of the hedgerows, you can't see the enemy. The front is fluid, and often you don't know whether the field next to you is occupied by friend or foe. It's like a huge game of cops and robbers, with all of the chips down, and our men find themselves chasing around in circles, trying to catch the enemy from the rear.

They rarely speak of having advanced a mile. Instead, it's

'We advanced eleven hedgerows,' or, 'We advanced eleven fields.' Normally, 'No man's land' is the width of a single field, but sometimes it's only the width of a single hedgerow. This happens after prolonged firing when both sides are regrouping and are too tired to move much. Then our men hear the Jerries talking a few feet away on the other side of the hedge.

This kind of warfare is right up the ally of the sniper, bazooka expert, and automatic-weapons handler. Conversely, it's death on tanks and armored cars, as scores of German vehicles burned to a peculiar shade of pink along the road give mute evidence. The destruction of equipment is appalling. Vehicles seldom get beyond the first soldier they meet who happens to be armed with a rifle grenade or bazooka. A tough young general's aide who goes up to the line to lead patrols ways, 'Give me ten infantrymen in this terrain, with proper combinations of small arms, and I'll hold up a battalion for 24 hours.'

The guy on the ground is the big man here, and there isn't much in the book to tell him what to do. He just uses what he's got and improvises. Right now, for instance, the infantrymen are employing an effective substitute for mortar fire. They fire rifle grenades at a high angle of elevation by firing their rifles from the ground, butts down. The grenade is fused for five seconds. It describes a high arc, traveling forward about 200 feet, and then at the end of the five seconds explodes in the air over the heads of the Germans, who are sheltered from the bursts from the front and sides. This airburst fragmentation is usually fatal. One rifle-grenade-man in this sector once used his weapon to eliminate an enemy sniper. He spotted the German in an apple tree, crawled up to within a 40-foot range, and let go at the back of the German's helmet. The Nazi disintegrated.

Throughout the fighting, French farmers and their families live in holes dug in cellars while their houses are destroyed over their heads. When the fighting passes beyond them, or during lulls, children come out to play and farmers bring butter and eggs to the GIs.

These lulls are necessary in hedgerow warfare. After a certain number of hours of advancing through fields, both sides are so worn out that he soldiers must stop to rest, regroup, and gather up the dead and wounded. The word 'lull' is a misnomer, course. Snipers keep on working, mortar and artillery shells plop down, and patrols go out at night. But it's like Sunday in Central Park compared to what's gone before. It was during one of these lulls that I moved up to the front.

The unit I was with---the 29th Division---had launched a big attack the day before to capture high ground dominating the big hedgehog city of St. Lo from the east.

The men had advanced all day and occupied the villages of St. Andre de L'Epine and Martinville, cutting the main highway from Bayeux to St. Lo. During the night, they reached their objective and stopped to allow another unit on the right flank to catch up. All night the artillery blasted in our ears. The 105s cracked, seemingly in the next field. Farther back, the Long Toms banged with their deep bass tones and shells went rushing overhead like fast freights passing tiny way-stations on the Pennsylvania Railroad line. It's amazing how you learn to sleep through such artillery barrages--- that is when the stuff is going in the right direction. (*Yank,* Sgt, Bill Davidson, Aug. 6, 1944)

These articles were all the information she had about his situation in the war. For her, like the rest of the loved ones at home, there was very little communication about what was taking place in the war.

The boxcar hit a bump. He was jerked back to his present reality when he noticed that most of the other troops in the boxcar were becoming very attentive and curious as they tried to absorb what had happened and speculate on their futures. They had heard so many rumors about the invasion and conditions on the front lines.

The front lines had an unusual pseudo-romantic mystique and ambivalence. The mystique centered on, for many involved in the war effort, excitement vs. death, action vs. inaction, arcane vs. mundane, notoriety vs. anonymity, fighting vs. supporting the fighters. Many support troops stationed behind the lines wanted to visit or see the front lines so they could claim they were where the action was taking place in the war, even though they weren't in direct combat with the enemy. In France, he had several requests from divisional command for support personnel to visit the front lines. He didn't like being responsible for their well-being when they visited. He generally regarded the requests as a pain in the ass. Nevertheless, what irritated him the most was to see rear echelon troops wearing campaign ribbons, which he and his men had never seen. When this happened in a bar, a near riot would usually follow, with anywhere from one to a dozen of his soldiers in jail or a stockade for the night.

Sitting among them, as they headed toward their destiny and their first taste of combat, was a person who had been in combat. They looked at him like they were seeing a rare bird. He could tell they were scared, apprehensive, and overcome with dread but terrifyingly naïve. The replacements had been transferred around from induction centers to training centers to replacement pools. Finally, at last, they were headed for action at the front, for better or worse. For the first time since they entered an induction center, they now had a clear mission, genuine unit association, and combat identity. They would be fighting with a regular unit with frontline officers. He knew what they were experiencing because he had been a replacement officer, without any combat experience, in the invasion of France. Now he was a rare bird. He was a replacement officer, once again, with decorated combat experience. This time, he knew what to expect, life, death, or insanity.

He was well aware of what veteran combat soldiers thought about replacement troops.

Eventually, you don't expect anything. I mean you give up. At first, the old bunch who are left are no longer bitter as they were in their second and third hitches.

'Resigned' is a better word to describe them now.

These kids, these reinforcements, they always think we'll be called back to a rest area or get furloughs in Paris or be rotated or have two weeks in England or be relieved or something.

'Dream on,' I tell them, 'dream on.' I used to think about going home-----two years ago. Like we used to have a saying, 'What do you expect-----eggs in your beer?' Now we say, 'What do you expect------beer?' What a joke! (*Yank, the Army Weekly,* May 25, 1945)

Earlier in the spring, the coast of France had been green, lush, and a lot warmer. Now the weather was cold and overcast as they headed for the Rhineland. They were bone-chillingly cold. It started raining harder. The passing fields were partially flooded.

They could see hundreds of military vehicles stuck in the deep mud all along the way.

The war looked to them like a muddy mess more than anything else, not exciting or glorious, just mud.

He thought, *this trip back to the front is turning out to be as cold and miserable as the Louisiana maneuvers at Fort Polk last year, and that was the coldest I've ever been. Nobody was shooting at me then, but the Germans will be again like they did in France after the invasion.*

Am I ready for this?..............................Are Skip and the boys warm and safe?...................................Am I ready for this?..............................The hospital rattled my nerves and I've got doubts about going back in.

When he went in on the fifth day of the invasion as a replacement captain, he knew he would be replacing a company commander of a heavy weapons company, which was equipped with mortars and machine guns. He also knew he would be replacing a previous captain who was either killed or wounded in the invasion. He was scheduled to command H Company of the 29th Division. The 29th was advancing toward and preparing to attack St. Lo. The Germans were fighting furiously to defend all the approaches to the city. He caught up with his outfit at St. Clair-Sur-L'Elle. The company clerk's entry in the daily report was:

Shearer, Robert L. capt. 116 13th June 44 to duty as CO.

St. Lo was being defended, on its western approach where he was, by veteran German 3ʳᵈ Division paratroopers, so his memories of France, his first time in combat, were not pleasant. Most of the troops that arrived as replacements were young, untested, and innocent, a force that didn't appear to have much of a chance of surviving against the veteran German fighters. Many didn't survive.

The rumor he heard back in England was that eventually over ten thousand American troops were killed at St. Lo. The turnover rate in his platoons had been over seventy–five percent. When the replacements were sent up to join his company to fill the ranks, they came without any orientation about what was taking place on the front lines. He really never had a chance to organize the platoons into an organized fighting team. He knew this was why casualties among the new recruits were so terribly high. He knew it would be this way again in the Rhineland.

His memories of France were also not good ones because, in addition to being wounded there, he had almost been killed several times. He had been very lucky, and he didn't see how mathematically he could get that lucky again.

The first close brush with death occurred between the two small towns of St. Clair and Villers Fossard when a mortar shell exploded behind him. One large piece of shrapnel glanced off the back of his helmet. Another smaller piece hit him in the butt. Fortunately, it hit his leather wallet and pierced several different layers of leather but stopped before hitting his skin. The wallet was still in his pocket as he rode the train back to the front, and it was a constant reminder of the randomness and reality of being wounded in battle.

The second time occurred at St. Clair. There was a lull in the fighting at St. Clair when he arrived. He had set up his command post in a privy behind a vacant house.

He was standing in front of the vacant house when a sniper's bullet whizzed between himself and Major Cawthon, his executive officer. It was also hard to think about St. Clair because one of his Lieutenants, named "Panko," was killed in the graveyard behind the church of Notre Dame. He was killed by a sniper who was in one of the buildings in the city.

But the incident that he couldn't get off his mind occurred at Villers Fossard. He, Lieutenant Talbot, and Major Cawthon had entered a stone smokehouse and found a German mess kit and a half-eaten ham. He and Lieutenant Talbot, who was from Massachusetts, half jokingly argued about who was going to check the second-floor of the smokehouse. Major Cawthon stayed on the ground floor, trying to locate their position on a mud-smudged map. Lieutenant Talbot prevailed and proceeded to climb the ladder on the outside wall to the second-floor loft, and he had asked him for his rifle because from his vantage point, he saw a German soldier in a hedgerow. He handed him his Garand rifle because Lieutenant Talbot had a carbine, with which you couldn't hit a distant target.

The floor had gaps in the floorboards so he could see him as he checked the second floor for enemy soldiers. A sudden blast of rifle fire hit the smokehouse, and Lieutenant Talbot fell to the floor above. Blood began to drip from the floorboards above. About the same time, three G.I. riflemen ran up to the front door of the smokehouse and announced they had just killed a German soldier on the second floor.

He glared at them and said, "The hell you did. You just killed the best officer I've ever had!" When he and the major went upstairs, Lieutenant Talbot was dead. He had never gotten over the incident. In fact, it had haunted him in the hospital in England and triggered some very bad bouts with anxiety. What made the incident so painful was that the very next day the regiment lost thirty-five men, another officer, and two first sergeants, to friendly fire from their own artillery. He knew the poor bastards didn't have a chance.

A strange, bizarre, and disconcerting close call happened between St. Clair and Villers Fossard. The company came upon a large French chateau that seemed rather intact for a structure in a war zone. When they went up to the door, a French lady appeared who was rather well-dressed. She invited them in for dinner. They went in and she set places for the men and brought out the food.

They noticed that the people that lived there, an old French family, appeared to be quite aristocratic. There were large paintings on the wall and war accommodations received by family ancestors. The home was well-appointed and seemed to have, remarkably, escaped any hint of destruction from either side in the war.

Just as they were about to eat, American artillery opened up, and shells started exploding in the orchard next to the chateau. They dropped to the floor and quickly left, leaving the food on the table, and made their way away from the artillery fire. When they got to Couvains, the next town, they asked the villagers about the chateau, and the villagers threw their hands in the air and exclaimed "collaborateurs, collaborateurs." They were glad they didn't eat the meal that could have been poisoned.

His month in France ended on the eleventh day of July. H Company along with the rest of the surrounding units was set to launch a major attack on St. Lo at daybreak. The attack involved twelve divisions in four corps attacking along a twenty-five-mile front. St. Lo was important because it was the first major city blocking a breakout from the beach invasion. The Germans were defending the city and its approaches because it was an apex of a road net that led in all directions. It was also the provincial seat of government and a major objective that had to be taken if the invasion was to continue to move inland.

He had set up the mortars and machine guns across the road from the command post. He was supposed to have eight machine guns and six 81mm mortars but one of the mortars did not have a base plate which rendered it useless. Also, because of the storms on the beach that reduced the ammunition supply, they were allocated three 81mm mortar shells per mortar tube per day. They were allotted two hundred and fifty rounds of .30 caliber machine gun ammunition.

Prior to the attack, he had taken a picture of his fellow officers sitting on a burned-out German command car opposite the battalion command post. Lieutenant Shepard, Lieutenant Raggett, Lieutenant Harvey, Lieutenant Woodworth, Lieutenant Noble, Lieutenant Hill, and Captain Murphy and he posed for the picture.

Lieutenant Hill was killed a short time later. Lieutenant Hill had been leading a platoon positioned about one hundred and fifty yards to his left. The platoon was approaching a slight rise in the landscape when they encountered a German bunker. He heard the small arms fire erupt, but he was confident the platoon could take out the bunker without additional support from another platoon. He was moving forward without any resistance. The small arms fire stopped and he could see a white flag being waved by the Germans in the bunker, indicating surrender.

For a few minutes there was a quiet period and then the small arms fire intensified at a serious level, so he figured he better get over where there was trouble. The platoon had just stopped shooting when he arrived. They had killed all of the Germans in the bunker. Lieutenant Hill was also dead. The men explained that when the Germans emerged from the bunker single file, the soldier in the lead, holding the white flag, dropped to his knees and the soldier directly behind him was holding a submachine gun. The second soldier shot Lieutenant Hill from a few feet away, and then the platoon rushed the bunker and killed all of the Germans with concentrated fire on the bunker after they had taken firing positions. They were not as close as the officer, and it took a few minutes for the fighting to end.

When he gathered Lieutenant Hill's dog tags and personal effects, he found that the Germans had, in the brief period before they had been subsequently killed, already taken the officer's watch and ring before he could get himself over to the commotion and see what had happened. The theft really made him angry, and he was in disbelief that they had done it so quickly and with the awareness that they were going to die shortly. He was still mad about the incident.

Lieutenant Raggett was later killed at Vire, France. He wasn't sure what happened to the others. He had an X-ray technician develop the picture in the hospital after he was wounded and evacuated. He sent the picture home, but the image of the group was still on his mind.

The attack on St. Lo began shortly before 6 o'clock in the

morning of July 11th. The American artillery barrage began with the sounds of hundreds of thumps behind them, which meant shells were being fired at the city and the attack had begun. The shells whizzed overhead and created explosions all along the German positions. Salvo after salvo crashed on the German positions. Machine guns were firing and the tanks moved forward. The noise was deafening. After the artillery fire subsided, the rifle companies were supposed to move forward. They were soon greeted by the reply of German machine guns that seemed to be untouched by the artillery barrage that had just pounded their positions.

H company was supposed to move along the sunken Bayeux–St. Lo road near St. Andre de-L' Epine. On the morning of the 11[th,] a sniper shot him, his orderly, Private Shearer, and Lieutenant Shepard at seven o'clock in the morning. Private Eugene Shearer was killed instantly, shot in the heart. A machine gun killed Lieutenant Shepard. The next bullet that got him after the private was killed, passed through and severed his pistol belt and hit his hip. It missed bones and vital organs but created a large flesh wound.

"When you got hit captain,……..Did it hurt?……. I mean, what was it like?" one of the young soldiers in the boxcar asked. He was hesitant to ask but also very curious.

"It was like someone smacking you with the flat side of a two-by-four. It didn't hurt…until later, and then it hurt like hell. The worst part was I lost my Singer .45."

The Singer Sewing Machine Company was one of the manufacturers of the .45 caliber pistol. He thought the pistol was the highest quality made among the various manufacturers. He got the holster back after the war, but not the pistol. When he was hit, he grabbed for his left hip, but the bullet hit him on the right hip. He had dreamed the night before he was going to get shot on his left side, but the wound was on the right side. Bleeding from his right hip, he crawled two hundred yards away from the front lines and, by chance, stumbled into an aid station. He didn't know where the aid station was located, but he knew he had to get one and away from the sniper. Instead of crawling down the open road, which would have been much easier, he crawled through a briar patch or thicket. It was a long way to crawl on his hands and knees. Without a doubt, he didn't want to give the sniper another clear shot at him, so he took the route that reduced that possibility. It also was much rougher on him, because he endured the frequent thorns tearing at his uniform and bare skin. At the aid station, he was bandaged and given a shot of morphine and an application of sulfa drugs. He was then prepared to be evacuated back to the beach.

"Where are we headed captain?" one of the young troops asked.

"Well, I think most of us are headed for the Rhineland. I'm supposed to report to Herleen, Holland. That's where there is a "Repple Depple" (replacement depot) if the Germans haven't blown it to hell by now."

He knew there wouldn't be anybody left from his old unit in France. The 29th had been in continuous action since he had left and was almost to the German border, crossing France, Belgium, and Holland, but the division had suffered heavy casualties.

Moving to the front had been a slow process, and the front lines could be located anywhere by the time the troops got to their units. He had looked at maps, and it appeared he was going to be going to be headed to Leige, Belgium as he was now, and then to Herleen, Holland because Herleen was in American control, but the German Army wasn't far beyond Herleen.

He knew he could suppress any emotional trouble until he heard the sound of explosions. Then the fear would set in, manifested by his stomach drawing into a knot. He had seen in the hospitals in England the ravages of explosive ordnance on the human body. Seared into his memory were the images of hundreds of soldiers, blinded, maimed, and burned. He had seen hundreds of amputees and hundreds more with combat fatigue. He had seen the ones, who had not died from shrapnel wounds, with red cuts and scars all over their bodies from being hit with smaller pieces of shrapnel. They looked like they had been cut in random locations on their bodies with a knife.

In the hospital, he had heard their crying, screaming, and moaning. He had smelled the odor of blood mixed with antiseptics. He had seen the orderlies and nurses dashing around the wards at night trying to keep soldiers from killing themselves.

In addition, he had seen orderlies removing the bodies of soldiers who had died during the night. Still more ravaged soldiers arrived to fill the empty hospital spaces to witness or participate in the macabre guerilla theater of death. It went on night after night.

At one point he couldn't take it any longer. He had tried to suppress all of the horrible images, but they occasionally bubbled up into his awareness. He had trouble sleeping at night. He had reoccurring flashbacks when he was awake. He knew his "nerves were shot" and anxiety could overcome him at the slightest hint or provocation. It was too much to bear, and now he was looking straight into the eyes of some new candidates for the explosive ordnance to work its gruesome or deadly effects.

From the beach, he was flown on a C-47 transport airplane to an airfield in England. The truck ride to the beach had been long and rough, each bump wrenching his wound so that when he arrived on the beach, his bandages were soaked in blood. He was again given sulfa drugs and morphine. In England, he was placed in hospitals in Tidwouth and Southampton. The company clerk's entry into the daily report was:

Shearer, Robert L. capt. H 116 13th July 44 fr hosp to dropped from rolls

In the first hospital, he had surgery to get stitches for internal closure and then for final closure of the wound and a drain tube. The second hospital stay was for a period of observation, rehabilitation, and release. The food wasn't very good in any of the hospitals because there was a critical shortage in England due to the war. The English people didn't have much to eat, so the hospitals were short of food, but the food was much better than C-rations. He wrote the following letter:

July 20, 1944

My Dearest:

Well, they sewed me up this p.m. and by damn I hope I never

have to go thru that again. Fighting on the front is a picnic to going in that damn operating room. I hope having a baby was easier than that. If it wasn't, we'll have no more babies I think they took eight stitches and only partially closed it up. Now I'm immobilized as hell and I probably will be numb for a few days.

This will have to be a short one, hon. I can't write handily and I don't feel too good either. I love you hon and hope that I can get home to you soon.

All my love,
Bob

As the train of soldiers in overcoats moved toward Liege, Belgium, the weather got colder and the troops got agitated, cold, and stiff. Frostbite hadn't been a problem for him in France back in the spring, but he knew the men around him were uncomfortable and that their feet were numb because his were. As it got colder and the soldiers stood in trenches filled with water, frostbite and trench foot were to became a major problem in the winter fighting conditions in the Rhineland.

After about an hour, the train slowed and came to a stop in the middle of the countryside. At first, he didn't see any reason to stop. He guessed it was about sixty miles between the cities but the train was only going thirty to thirty–five miles an hour, so the trip was, he calculated, going to last about two hours.

As the soldiers climbed out of the line of boxcars he soon knew why they had stopped because of what he saw and smelled. The train had stopped for the troops to go to the bathroom. The train cars, obviously, had no bathroom facilities, so the stop was timely and needed. Several of the young soldiers lit C-ration cigarettes for a smoke.

It looked to him like all of the trains going back and forth to the front stopped at this peculiar place because the ground on both sides and in both directions was covered with empty C-ration cans, piles of human feces, and toilet paper left from previous visits to the cold, open-air latrine. Even in the cold, the odor was nauseating. He knew it would be much worse if the temperature wasn't so close to freezing. He immediately noticed all of the different kinds of toilet paper that had been used.

Most toilet paper came from C-rations, but soldiers quickly learned to stuff scraps of paper for later use into their pockets. They had to scrounge paper whenever and wherever they could. He grinned when he saw an occasional German or American propaganda leaflet that had been effectively and conveniently pressed into latrine duty.

After another hour, the train began to slow again and the men, seeing they were coming into Liege, began to stir. They were happy to be moving around so they could ward off the cold in their bodies and get off the wretchedly cramped boxcar. They were also apprehensive because they knew they were getting close to the front.

The train stopped in Liege and all of the troops scrambled out of the boxcars and were directed by MPs (Military Police) to several two–and–a–half ton trucks waiting a few blocks away. Each truck swallowed its capacity of twelve soldiers and headed toward Herleen in a long line, lurching and whining as the drivers shifted the gears of the big olive-drab colored trucks.

The "deuce and a halfs" as they were called, were covered with a canvas top, but they were just as cold as the boxcars, but much rougher riding. The cold rain and fog continued relentlessly. Leaving Liege, they crossed the recently reconstructed bridge over the Meuse River and headed for Herleen. As the long line of trucks approached the city, he could hear the rumble of artillery in the direction of the city. The other soldiers on the truck had heard it also and knew it wasn't thunder. He could tell they were apprehensive. This meant the front line was near and that they were getting close. The thunderous noise in the distance grew louder and he knew it came from German artillery. He knew the sound well. It would send shivers down your spine and put a knot in your stomach.

From the truck, he could see the long, flat terrain of the

Rhineland that stretched for miles. The landscape looked like land he had only seen in the American west, stretching for miles. The muddy fields were only interrupted by a series of villages, each of which had a church steeple. The Rhineland terrain was gray and bleak and appeared to be impossible to cross as the sight of many vehicles stuck in the mud confirmed.

It was the middle of November 1944, and he wondered where he would be by Christmas.

Before his mind could wander too far, a bump in the muddy road reminded him of the reality of the moment and that his emotions would be tested soon. The thunder of artillery in the distance got louder and he hoped the driver of the truck wouldn't stop and try to make them walk the rest of the way. He had heard of these altercations between truck drivers and troops before. Some of the drivers wanted nothing to do with the action on the front line.

Who could blame them?

In Herleen, the deuce and a halfs pulled in and stopped in front of the repple depple to unload. It was a converted technical high school. It was fully furnished and looked like the students had recently left their drafting tables. There was a big park in front of the school which was located on a broad city square. The cooking facilities were in the basement and the latrines were in the back yard of the school. The troops were sleeping in storerooms, on the floor, and on the drafting tables. As usual, the troops in the depot were smoking cigarettes, so the room was filled with smoke. All of them were waiting to move up to the front when they were needed to replace killed or wounded soldiers. The front line was close to the Holland-German border and the GIs had been fighting for the small towns between Herleen and the Roer River, including Koslar. A dozen of these small towns and villages dotted the flat plain that stretched to the Roer River. The Germans fought to hold each one in defense of the German border. In Herleen, he immediately reported to Lieutenant Colonel Cassell.

"Welcome to Herleen, captain."

He saluted and said, "It took a while to get here."

"We don't see many company commanders. Where did you come from?"

"The hospital in England. I was in the same hospital with Colonel Bingham. Is he here? He was the Battalion Commander back in France, you know?"

"Yeah, but I guess he hasn't made it back yet. You just missed General Eisenhower. He was here last week."

"This must be an important assignment."

"Well, he thought so."

"Okay, we're going to continue the attack to the east soon. Right now we're stuck here because of this damned weather. Reconnaissance planes are grounded as well as air support. We can't see what's ahead. Ike said for us to go forward in about two weeks even if the weather doesn't change."

He thought, *Damn! That means we will lose the air support. It means we will lose more men because the Germans will be free to move around and shoot at us while we slug through the mud which really slows soldiers down. And, we will have little intelligence provided by air reconnaissance. Shit! That sounds like a suicide mission.*

He paused and said, "In the meantime, I'm assigning you to be the Assistant S3, Battalion Operations Officer. We don't have much equipment, but as you can tell, the building is heated. The rumor going around is that back in the states, they think the war is over so they're not making any more mortar shells and ammunition. The truth is, we can't get much over these roads and we've outrun our supply line. In two weeks we'll be in better shape."

He added, "It looks like we squat here for about two weeks. See Sergeant Dones downstairs. He'll set you up. By the way, I guess you've noticed we're in range of artillery."

"Yeah, I couldn't miss it." He had noticed all of the shell craters in the fields around the town.

It wouldn't take much shelling to level this town, maybe one or two direct hits.

"Goddamned railway gun someplace. We only get shelled at night. Nobody seems to know where it is, and it only fires at night to avoid detection by our planes."

He then reported to the company clerk in the replacement depot. The company clerk's entry for that day read as follows:

Shearer, Robert L. capt. Hq 3 bn 29 Nov 44 from repl depot to dy as ass S 3
His next entry was:
Shearer, Robert L. capt. Hq 3 bn 29 Nov 44 atched for rations

The city continued to be shelled at night for the next two weeks while they waited on the weather to clear and be re-supplied. Living under the bombardment was nerve wracking because the shells from the big gun were landing in and around the town and leaving big holes in the old brick and stone buildings. The depot had not been hit, but he had heard the familiar sound of the shells passing overhead. All of the troops had trouble sleeping at night under the shelling.

They knew the gun could get lucky and hit the building. The only comforting thing about being there was that the 2nd Armored Division was bivouacked around Herleen. So, they were not likely to get overrun by a surprise German counterattack. The discomforting fact was that the tanks couldn't move through the mud either, especially where the enemy had dug deep water-filled anti-tank trenches. They could only move on the roads and not across fields.

After about a week he got relief from the bombardment when he requisitioned a jeep and went back to Brussels on a three-day pass. He had traded a Dutch family in Herleen some bacon drippings for a Voightlander camera. He had "requisitioned" the drippings and several cans of C-rations from the kitchen in the basement.

In the repple depple, he received three hot meals a day, including bacon and eggs for breakfast.

Rations

The quartermaster reveals that the 1943 dogface gets five times more fruits and vegetables in his daily rations than were issued to a soldier of the Continental Army of 1775---or 35 ounces against seven. But, here's the hitch; today's G.I. doesn't get the quart of spruce beer or hard cider

that the Colonial dogface received each day.
Daily rations of meat and milk were the same then
as now---a pound of meat and a pint of milk to each
enlisted man. Except, as our history books tell us, the
Continentals didn't get theirs as regularly as we do. (*Yank,*
Vol. 1,Mar 27, 1943)

Unfortunately, most of the civilians were hungry, and the family had children who were very hungry so they made the trade. He took the camera to Brussels and took pictures of the destruction of the city that he had seen passing through a few weeks earlier. He scrounged a dress uniform to wear back to Brussels. It was a bit too small, but it served the purpose.

He arrived in Herleen with a carbine which he thought was almost useless. He wanted to swap it for a second .45 automatic like he had carried and used many times earlier in action in France. The .30, M1 carbine fired a .30 caliber pistol bullet that dropped radically at two hundred yards so it was difficult to hit what was being shot at. The target had to be very close. He called it a "pea shooter." It had a slow muzzle velocity and wouldn't pierce armor plate.

The pistol was much quicker to bring into position, aim, and fire. It also had more knockdown power. Because of its maneuverability, the .45 was much better than the carbine for searching out buildings and houses, close range combat, and shooting quickly. Now, he set his mind on getting rid of his carbine in a trade. He wanted a second .45 before he got to the front because he knew he could hit what he was shooting at with the .45 automatic. Before the war, he had won many medals and trophies in Dallas, Austin, and Atlanta for pistol marksmanship using a .45 and other pistols.

He successfully traded his M1 carbine for another .45 pistol with a tank crew member named "Fish" he met in Herleen. Tank crew members were issued .45s, but many were eager to trade for a carbine because the carbine had a greater effective range that the pistol. They particularly liked the paratrooper carbine with a folding stock because it was easier to move around inside the tank but were happy to get any carbine.

He continued to look at the pictures of Skip at every chance he had when he was alone and out of the rain. He knew Herleen would be his last chance until he returned from the field because the conditions in the field could ruin or damage the pictures.

In addition to the extra .45, he had his pipe and tobacco pouch in the pockets of his field jacket, Skip's pictures in his billfold, several loaded spare .45 clips in his ammunition belt, and a pair of spare socks. He was now ready to go back to the frontlines.

Chapter Two

Koslar

THE TWO-AND-A-HALF TON TRUCK LOADED WITH twelve soldiers made different whines, groans, and grinding noises as the gears were shifted along the muddy road leaving Herleen. It was December 1st, 1944. The big trucks lurched and swayed on the irregular road, jostling and bouncing their loads of human cargo. The weather had not improved, and it had gotten colder. He was heading further across the Rhineland toward a small town called Koslar. Koslar had just been captured by the 29th and the army needed officers for the next phase of the November offensive. A series of small villages had fallen in the last week, and the line of trucks was passing through them. Setterich, Siersdorf, and Englesdorf were now in Allied hands. In Siersdorf, the trucks passed the Siersdorf castle which was now being used as a command post. He thought it looked like a castle, but it was old and stained with soot like old buildings he had seen in the big cities of the eastern United States.

The trucks passed groups of German soldiers being marched to rear areas. They had been captured or had surrendered in the battles across the Rhineland. He first saw small groups of ten to twelve prisoners and then large groups of fifty cold, disheveled, stooped, plodding, and ragtag prisoners. Some were bandaged from wounds suffered in battle. They seemed to have a doomed and depressed look on their faces because the German Army had told them they would be shot by the Americans if they were captured.

He had estimated it was fifteen to twenty miles from Herleen to Koslar. With the slow going of the trucks, he guessed the trip was going to take an hour if they didn't get stuck or stopped along the way. When the trucks got to Englesdorf, they could hear the artillery that was shelling Koslar. Most of the replacements got very agitated at being this close to the noise. He knew it would get more intense at night because the Germans did not want to get their artillery positions exposed to attack in the daytime by allied planes. The overcast skies had given the German artillery positions protection from the bombing threat up to this point.

Like all of the small towns, Koslar had been surrounded on the western approach with a system of deep anti-tank trenches, minefields, and barbed wire. The trenches had been dug by German civilians who had been pressed into service by the military home guard. Approaching Koslar, they could see the aftermath of the battle for control of the city. Like other towns he had seen on the trip, Koslar was utterly destroyed. It had been reduced to and consisted of piles of rubble with a road cleared through the debris for army vehicles to pass.

Most of the collapsed buildings had been flattened or blown asunder by heavy bombing. It reminded him of the destruction and aftermath of tornados he had seen in Texas and Oklahoma, only much worse. A few walls were standing, but household items were scattered around muddy yards among the dead cows, goats, pigs, and other livestock. Trees were shattered, charred, and splintered from the blasts of exploding mortar and artillery shells. The odor of the decaying animals was nauseating. The village church was unrecognizable. The graveyard had been cratered and pock marked by shells that left fragments of tombstones and buried coffins strewn about. All of the destruction was the result of a cataclysmic ordnance arms-ageddon which few cities avoided in the advance of allied forces. Four American tanks could be seen off to the right of the road. They were knocked out, burned, and disabled. Their separated metal tracks were lying in the mud like the tails of dead dragons. The retreating German artillery had been hitting the town and pummeling surrounding areas to prevent American soldiers and supplies from reaching it. Likewise, American artillery had been hitting the town to gain control. He could tell there had been a helluva fight for control of Koslar.

As soon as he entered the outskirts of the city, he saw a group of prisoners and their captors. Beyond the rubble and discarded German equipment sat the prisoners and their flat-faced captors standing guard. The prisoners had been captured in the battle for the city and surrounding areas. The soldiers guarding the captors moved them to a clearing in front of a destroyed building that still had a wall standing that afforded the group some protection from the cold wind.

He immediately saw a lieutenant and a sergeant who appeared to be in command, and two of the interrogators. He stopped, and the lieutenant an sergeant recognized him as a higher ranking officer.

They both saluted and said, "Captain."

He saluted back and said, "Looks like you've got your hands full."

"Yes sir," the sergeant said.

He paused and added, "Yeah, we caught us some shit house rats."

"I see."

He decided to eavesdrop on the interrogations, linger and provide some command support for the outnumbered soldiers with rifles pointed at the captors. The lieutenant looked slightly relieved that there were now other American troops on the scene, especially another officer.

The collection of German prisoners reminded him of similar situations he had observed in France in the previous spring.

Damn! These prisoners are different. They're just a bunch of kids, old men, and civilians.

He soon learned from the interrogators that some of the prisoners weren't even German. He noticed what they said about the group. The huddled group consisted of soldiers and civilians. The soldiers were wearing German Army overcoats and steel helmets. The civilians were wearing a hodgepodge of garments for protection from the cold and rain. They were wearing blankets, tattered overcoats, and unrecognizable other forms of outerwear.

The interrogators were trying to communicate with the prisoners, but they only knew French and German. The soldiers with rifles pointed at the group were sitting on piles of rubble that they had found for a more comfortable perch. The interrogators weren't making much progress in the misting rain.

It soon became obvious some of the prisoners were Russian, Polish, and Yugoslavian. He had seen the same mix of prisoners from various countries when he was fighting in France. It seems that the German Army had pressed into military service a variety of soldiers from overrun countries.

What he saw was a very strained and tense standoff, more tense that usual prisoner detention situations. The tension was higher because the front line was very close and there was a very small American Army presence behind them. In effect, the captors were in custody, but the American forces were almost completely isolated and cut off from reinforcements. Furthermore, the German soldiers and civilians had been told that the Americans would shoot them if they were captured. That information added to their desperation.

On the other hand, the soldiers who had captured the prisoners were indifferent to the plight of the prisoners. They didn't care if they brought a prisoner into Koslar or killed him.

They're damn lucky they didn't shoot them.

He flashed back to scenes of German prisoners being shot in France. Most had been captured, but some were shot. He had hoped the scenes would fade from his memory. They hadn't.

Hardened combat soldiers had very little sympathy for hostile enemy soldiers. The soldiers guarding the prisoners in the rubble of Koslar could easily pull the trigger on their rifles like they had done thousands of times. Their language was the language of rifle fire.

He could see the prisoners sensed the peril they were in. They looked like frightened but resolved rabbits before the powerful jaws of a hungry wolf. Shooting was the way dogfaces communicated with strangers on the battlefield. In this tense scene, with language differences, all verbal communication had been abandoned. Fear, violence, and death were in the cold, drizzling air.

"Gawddamnit, shoot the sons a bitches!" he heard one of the soldiers say. He knew, and he could tell the interrogators knew that the captors could start shooting at any moment.

"Yeah, let's shoot em all."

He addressed the group, "At ease, soldier."

The group of soldiers guarding the prisoners looked impassively in his direction when they heard his order. He knew they hated officers, had seen a lot of men die and were battle weary. He knew they probably had seen enlisted men shoot American officers and German prisoners. They probably had seen their own men die from American artillery or mortar fire like he had seen. Their eyes were deep set and their faces showed the extreme strain of combat. He had seen many of them in the psychiatric wards in the hospitals in England when he was there. He had also seen many sitting in the fields in France waiting to be evacuated from the front line for the condition of shell shock. He hoped this group was scheduled to be rotated soon to a rear area. They were.

Knowing that some were suffering shell shock, he stayed on guard in the tense situation. He kept his hand on one of the .45 pistols on his hip because one of the soldiers could snap at any time.

All hell could break loose!

The impasse was broken when one of the interrogators noticed a man among the prisoners who was dressed in a ragged overcoat, striped shirt, black pants, and a black cap.

"What's that?" one of the soldiers asked, referring to the apparent civilian prisoner.

"I dunno. But, I'm going to try to see where he's from."

"He don't look like a soldier," one of the other soldiers guarding the group said.

A soldier from Seattle, who knew a little Russian, came into the clearing in the rubble and tried to speak to the hapless, frightened man. He kept his rifle pointed at the man during the attempted conversation.

The soldier from Seattle addressed the interrogators and said, "This guy claims he was captured by the Germans and moved to

Cologne to work. He's from Russia. He was working in Koslar. He managed to get away before we took the city and he's been hiding in the woods."

He continued to listen to the interaction between the soldiers, interrogators, and prisoners. He fully expected them to start shooting them if anything went wrong. He thought he'd better stay until they started marching the prisoners to the rear.

"I'll bet he hates that son of a bitch Hitler too," said one of the infantrymen.

"Ask him if he was a Russian soldier or a civilian when he was captured by the Germans."

"Let me shoot him first!"

The prisoner started jabbering, and the translating soldier said, "He claims he was a Russian soldier and was captured in the Ukraine."

"He shore don't look like no soldier." The prisoner pointed toward a sheet of paper and a pencil held by one of the interrogators.

On the paper he wrote, "1941."

"Ask him what he did before he got in the army."

The translator asked, and the man made a motion of someone swinging a scythe as the rain dripped from his cap when he moved from side to side.

The prisoner said, "Kolkhoz."

"He's lying!"

The translator said, "He worked on a big farm."

The soldier from Seattle then gave the man a cigarette. The rest of the infantrymen with rifles pointed at the group were stoic and unimpressed with the new information.

"Let's turn em over to the MPs and get the hell out of here!"

After he started smoking the cigarette, the prisoner began to show a faint smile. He now sensed he wasn't going to be shot.

He could tell the tense moment had passed so he was ready to head through the town to find the command post. Most of the soldiers guarding the prisoners had found a place to sit under an overhang and out of the misting rain. They could now enjoy a moment of peace, smoke a cigarette, get some rest, and catch a few moments of sleep.

Just as he was leaving, he heard one of the soldiers who captured the prisoners say, "Will one of you fuckers tell me what the hell is the sense in this business?" He had asked himself the same question many times. He had arrived at the same answer that the group provided the soldier who asked it, no answer.

Koslar was a small town with one main street that lay on the west side of a railroad track that ran north and south. The Germans had originally defended Koslar as the American Army advanced with artillery, but eventually relinquished the city without an aggressive ground contest and withdrew their forces back across the River Roer. The river marked the first natural barrier blocking entry into Germany.

There were two reasons why they relinquished the city. First, they were short of soldiers because Hitler was, unknown to the American Army, massing German troops further to the south for a winter counterattack. That counterattack became known as the "Battle of the Bulge." Second, with its natural river barrier and man-made fortifications, it was easier to defend. Nevertheless, the defenders that were left in Julich to defend the city were mostly boys and older men in the home guard, but they were well-armed fierce defenders.

East of the city and across the railroad tracks stood a complex of large brick buildings that had previously been a paper mill. It now was mostly in ruins and the roof had caved in, but the walls were still standing. The paper mill was still an imposing structure that overlooked the river plain to the east that led to the Roer River and a city on the other side of the river. On the high ground on the other side of the river, lay the city of Julich. The German Army was fortifying the resistance and preparing to prevent allied troops from crossing the river and entering their homeland.

The trucks loaded with armed soldiers slowly rolled along the muddy roads leading to Koslar. The drivers stopped short of the city, wanting little to do with the German 88s (88-millimeter artillery gun) hitting the city, especially their truck. All of the troops were from the 29th and were ordered to report to various company assignments after their hike through the city. They had all drawn rations and extra ammunition at the repple depple in Herleen. They were ready to fight, and they were about to get a chance very soon.

Some of the troops were like him, older men of the division who has been wounded earlier and were returning to their old outfits. They were strangers who rarely recognized anybody. They would ask about people they had previously known, but in war, a short time can change all the relationships among the troops. Very few soldiers knew anyone around them from previous combat assignments.

The MPs (Military Police) at the checkpoint on the edge of town told the replacements that all of the 29ers were dug in around the paper mill and that's where they needed to report for duty.

"Captain, the Battalion Command Post (CP) is in a bomb shelter in the basement of the paper mill," the MP said as he saluted.

"Go straight down the main street and it will be a group of buildings to your right, east of town along a railroad track."

"Thanks, corporal," he said as he saluted back.

He and the others headed down the main street and across a field to the paper mill southeast of the city. It was the afternoon of December 1st and it was raining, and thick mud clung to the shoes of all the troops after they left the streets of Koslar. He guessed it was about thirty-eight to forty degrees in the daytime, so he was sure it would be freezing at night. The clothes he was wearing would have to keep him warm in the open air, day and night. He was guardedly confident that his wool overcoat and pants would keep him from freezing. On the other hand, he knew he and his men wouldn't survive the cold if they got wet. He knew about trench foot casualties in the Rhineland campaign. From what he had seen in the hospital, the specter of the condition was omnipresent in cold and wet conditions.

When he arrived at the paper mill, troops were dug in around the west side of the old brick buildings, trying to stay out of the line of fire and the impact zone of the 88s. Several of them were smoking C-ration cigarettes. The paper mill had been hit and some of the second story windows were blown out. Part of the roof was missing, but it was in otherwise good shape considering how much explosive ordnance had landed on and around it.

He went down the stairs into the lower floor of the mill, moving around the debris scattered all over the floor of the brick buildings. The odor of mildew and rotting organic material was strong because the roof had leaked down into the building and turned piles of paper and pressed sugar beet pulp into a wet grey mush. The rooms smelled dank, musty, and sulfurous. There were smaller rooms leading away from the cavernous mill, and the CP was dimly lit in one of the more protected rooms at the rear. Not much light made it into the building so the CP was illuminated by kerosene lanterns.

When he entered the CP, he saw Colonel Bingham, much to his surprise.

As he saluted the major he said, "Captain Shearer reporting for duty, sir."

Colonel Bingham saluted back and said, "Hello captain. Haven't seen you since the hospital."

"How the hell did you get here before I did? I didn't see you in Herleen."

"I came straight through last night and relieved Colonel Cassell. Jeeps make better time than the deuce-and-a-halfs."

"What are we looking at, out ahead of us?"

"Well, we don't know much, but the Germans have pulled back to Julich and are hitting us with 88s, especially at night."

"We've been ordered to attack tomorrow, the second, so get your men into defensive positions for the night, and we will have a briefing at 8:00 am in the morning."

"It looks like it's all gonna happen pretty quickly."

"Yeah. Regimental command thinks we've waited long enough."

"Captain Shearer, you are assigned as the company commander for L Company. Two other captains are in charge of G and I companies. I'll introduce you to them at the briefing in the morning."

"In the meantime, watch out for those 88s."

"Yeah."

He saluted and headed back up to exit the building. He thought sarcastically, *Yeah! I'll watch out for the damned 88s. How is that done? If you hear one it probably is not going to get you. If you don't hear it, it won't make any difference because you won't hear anything else..............ever. He had heard the shells scream over his head before and knew they could scare the bejesus out of anybody. Shit! I'll watch out for them, yeah. I'll watch them kill a lot of these new replacement soldiers.*

He went back outside the building and located L Company huddled and partially dug in along the back wall of the mill. A brief count of the men gave him a sinking feeling. Instead of a full company of one hundred and twenty to one hundred and thirty men, there were only fifty very young replacements. It looked like two platoons, not four platoons. He also didn't see any officers that could serve as his platoon leaders. In fact, he only saw soldiers with the rank of private and only one with the rank of corporal. He also quickly realized this was a rifle company. He didn't see any mortars or machine guns, but fortunately, there was a BAR with a crew.

He thought, *What the hell is going on here? This company is seriously under-strength and under-supplied. The situation isn't looking very damn good at this point. In fact, this is nuts.....................to attack entrenched German positions without the support of machine guns and mortars. The only ammo we'll have is what we can carry. There won't be any chance of resupply. This is a helluva kettle of fish!*

Infantry Lacks Replacements

Already suffering from munition and tire shortages, American western front forces are now handicapped by a shortage of trained infantry replacements. Instead of there being a steady flow of replacements for the U.S. men are being taken from divisions on quiet sectors to meet deficiencies of divisions suffering heavy battle casualties.

As yet, the replacement shortage has not seriously impaired

the overall fighting efficiency of General Eisenhower's forces, but it has caused unnecessary headaches to local commanders. (*The Stars and Stripes,* Vol. 5, No. 39, Dec. 16, 1944)

The men in Company L had seen him in the mill, and they were still surprised when he got to where they were huddled along the wall. He recognized some of the men who had been in the boxcar with him on the way to the front lines.

"I'm Captain Shearer and I'm your new company commander. Who's the highest ranking soldier among you?"

The men saluted and looked around at each other and one said, "Corporal Jones is, sir."

"Anybody here a sergeant?"

None of the huddled group of soldiers responded.

"Okay corporal, you come with me, and we're going to look for a place to dig in before it gets dark."

As soon as he assumed command, he searched his memory to think how he should lead the men. He'd been out of command of any soldiers for some time, so he needed to go over in his mind what he needed to do. When he was fighting in France, he had lieutenants who directly commanded the troops. There weren't any lieutenants here for this attack. He soberly knew the reason why there weren't any junior officers available. The thought of why, how, and where so many had died left a permanent hole in his consciousness that stayed with him from day to day. They had been so alive, and then in an instant, they didn't exist. He wasn't able to suppress the shock of the losses.

He remembered he needed to be stoic, calm, confident, and firm in his commands and decisions. He knew he had to remain stoic in his appearance. All he was responsible for was killing Krauts and keeping his men alive. He wasn't their mother, babysitter, or best friend. He also remembered he had to remain calm emotionally and not rattled by the confusion and fog of battle and the sight of dead and mangled soldiers.

By the time he took command this time, most of the soldiers

knew he was a seasoned combat officer, so the question of his toughness under fire wasn't questioned by the young soldiers. He detected they were a little awestruck by having a captain in command instead of a green, untested, shave tail second lieutenant who could get them killed in an instant.

He and the corporal trudged and splashed through the muck around the mill and then east down along the brick wall to get a better view of the terrain beyond the mill. The mud around the old brick building was between ankle and calf deep. Then, they headed for the railroad embankment. The railroad embankment ran south from the mill. They crouched down and walked along the west side of the tracks, away and protected from German artillery. It looked to him like a good place to dig foxholes and launch their attack across the fields toward the *Sportplatz*. It was drier than the surrounding ground because it was elevated. That meant the holes wouldn't fill with water, and the soldiers could keep their feet dry before they headed into the muddy fields. He wanted them to start the attack with dry feet. It also afforded some revetment from incoming artillery coming from the east. He saw heavy wooden crates stacked in intervals along the tracks, but didn't pay any attention to them.

Looking across the river plain he said, "Okay corporal, go bring the company out here so we can get dug in before dark."

"Yes sir, captain. They're not gonna like leaving the protection of the mill sir."

"Yeah, I know, but this is where we're gonna be."

He knew the men would rather be protected by the mill, but he knew what could happen if German or allied planes decided to level it. He had become wary of buildings in France during his first time in battle. He knew they were treacherous, lethal, and unstable. They could collapse at any time with a falling wall, killing or injuring several soldiers at a time. He had been in the hospital with a soldier in a full body cast as a result of a wall collapsing on him. Maggots were put into the cast at the top and he and other patients picked them off when they came out of the cast around the man's ankles. The maggots removed old, dead, or decaying flesh under the cast. Also, he had scratched the man's feet because the itch was unbearable, and the soldier obviously couldn't accomplish the task himself.

Just then he thought he better get back to the mill and make sure the corporal returned with all of the few men under his command he had because the corporal probably had no previous command experience. He met the group coming along the wall of the mill when it was almost dark.

"Okay, let's get over to the railroad and get dug in," the corporal said.

"Come on corporal. We don't want to dig another hole," one of the soldiers said.

The company was reluctant to move away from the shelter of the building. All of the men were lined up along the wall. He could hear them muttering "Damn," Shit," and "Fuck," and other banal, profane, and scatological terms in protest of the corporal's order. He had heard all of the colorful language before and was, on occasion, to use some of the words. But, when it came to the amount and variety of swear words, enlisted men were highly creative and very uninhibited. He expected their protestations, lip, and recalcitrance. He then heard them throwing their entrenching shovels against the wall of the paper mill.

"Whaaaaaam!" A tremendous explosion erupted on the top of the wall where they were standing. He and most of the GIs were knocked to the ground by the exploding 88 shell. The explosion caused parts of the building to rain down on them. They were covered with bricks, mortar, and dust. The shell had hit the top of the second story and left a jagged gaping hole in the wall. He heard a lot more cussing as the GIs got up and shook the debris off their wet overcoats. Their overall color had changed from dark green to tan and brown from the coating of mortar, brick, and concrete dust.

That's good. They're cussing the Germans and not me anymore.

"Look to see if anybody got hit by any shrapnel corporal. Go down the line and check."

After a few minutes, he came back and reported nobody had gotten hit, but two had been briefly dazed from the concussion of the exploding shell and subsequent falling bricks.

"Okay, let's go."

At this point, the company of soldiers was not as reluctant to leave the safety of the brick building. The company made their way to the railroad embankment and started digging foxholes in the western slope along the elevated tracks.

It was dark now, and the digging was slow because the railroad bed had been packed down in order to lay the ties and rails. But, at least the holes were dryer than the surrounding fields. Consequently, the bottoms of the holes they were about to spend the night in wouldn't fill with water.

Trench foot cheated so far!

He told two of the men to dig their foxholes on the eastern side of the tracks so the whole group wouldn't be surprised by a German patrol at night. The rest of the company started digging on the western side. He told all of the men they could go back to the mill during the day to stay out of the rain. They had to be in their holes at night because that's when the shelling would take place. Being positioned along the west side of the slope would give them maximum protection because the railroad tracks were raised at least twelve feet above the surrounding partially flooded beet fields.

Colonel Bingham also sent a private to the third floor of the mill to watch the German lines from a higher place of observation. He was a lookout just in case the Germans made any surprise advances and counterattacked during the daytime. Fortunately, they didn't.

It was completely dark now with overcast skies. A light drizzle was falling. The company started digging among the large wooden crates that were scattered along the embankment. He decided to dig his foxhole under one of the crates.

What tha hell difference does it make? If an 88 hits me in the open, in a foxhole, or under this crate, I'll be dead in all cases!

He thought it would make a nice roof to keep the rain out of his hole. He managed to get the hole dug completely under the crate by 11:00 p.m. and subsequently collapsed into the hole from exhaustion. He had forgotten how tiring it was to dig a hole large enough to protect one person. It quickly brought back memories of France.

He remembered he had started digging a foxhole the previous spring, when he was fighting in France, late in the evening. He dug down about six inches and hit bedrock. He was so damned tired, he fell over and went to sleep with only a partially dug hole. When he awoke in the morning he discovered to his amazement that he had tried to dig his hole over an unexploded five hundred pound English bomb that was buried deep in the earth. A crashed British bomber had left the surprise, and the parts of the bomber were scattered over the entire area. He radioed back to send a demolition team up the front to detonate the bomb. When the detonation team got to the site, the sergeant in charge told him that the area must be cleared for at least a thousand yards in all directions. He told the sergeant that was a pretty amusing and ridiculous request since the German Army was positioned only a hundred yards away. The sergeant turned a little pale, and quickly, soberly, and diligently completed the task of exploding the bomb. He occasionally glanced furtively in the direction of the front lines of battle.

The German soldiers no doubt heard the explosion and the sergeant was no doubt a little shook up, apprehensive, and worried about being in range of a German sniper. Even though he was exhausted, he still had trouble getting to sleep in the first hole he had dug since fighting in France. He hated it then and he hated it now.

If I ever get out of this, I'm never going to sleep on the ground again!

He could tell the soldiers dug in around him were not asleep. Eavesdropping, he could hear parts of their conversations coming from his left, right, and the east side of the embankment where the point men were located.

To his left he heard, "I wish to hell I knew what we were supposed to do tomorrow."

And he heard, "Give me a kick if you see anything...just anything."
Then he heard, "When are we gonna be relieved?"
From a different soldier he heard, "What's the countersign in

case we have to get out of here?"

Another soldier replied, "I don't know. It doesn't make any difference anyway. If we tried to go back to the mill, the captain would shoot us first and ask questions later. We'll have to stay here until the attack."

To his left, he heard, "If we do have to get out of here for some reason, run back and yell as loud as you can 'captain I'm coming back.' He'll let you through------maybe."

And he heard, "Why didn't someone put some concertinas and trip flares in front of this hole? We wouldn't have to worry so much."

Then he heard, "Are the Germans going to shoot us if we have to move out of these gawdamned holes?"

From close to the previous conversation, he heard, "Just pee into that cup I found at the mill and throw it over the tracks."

Finally, to the east of where he was, he heard. "Take a look into my sector every once in a while. I'm not certain I can see at all."

Another soldier exclaimed, "God, that dead pig smells bad!"

Then another said, "I can't see a damned thing."

The soldiers to the east had the following conversation, "You ever kill anybody?"

"No, you?"

"Sheeeeeeeeit, no!"

Daylight revealed that the company was dug in along a hundred yard stretch of railroad embankment. Daylight also revealed that the wooden crate he had dug under was a crate of live 88 shells.

He muttered to himself, "What the hell is going on here? " When he looked along the embankment, he could see all the other crates were filled with live 88 shells, lined up to supply the big guns that the German Army used to terrorize the advancing Americans. What puzzled him was that this railroad track ran north and south, not east and west, so the Germans didn't intend the shells for the cities to the east.

The only thing he could figure was that they had been planning a major offensive, north or south of where they were before the Americans had overrun the supply line. The Germans obviously had not had enough time to rescue the crates of shells before they retreated.

But why would they want them south of his position? Everything north of where they were had been in Allied hands for some time. They must have been planned for action to the south of Koslar. I better get the information back to command headquarters if the Germans had originally planned a major offensive.

Before the early briefing, he wanted to scan the countryside beyond their positions with his field glasses. He lay down on the protected side of the tracks and scanned the river bottom leading up to the Roer River. It was 7:30 a.m. and he didn't have much time before the briefing. It didn't make much difference because through the fog and rain he couldn't see a damned thing. What he could see was a gently sloping hill leading away from the railroad tracks parallel to two roads. In the distance, closer to the river, he could see the outline of the higher ground on the other side of the river and the silhouette of a city.

What he could see, that made chill bumps rise on his back, was that anyone who tried to cross the open fields would be sitting ducks for German mortars and machine guns. As a company commander of a heavy weapons company, it was a terrain situation that gave the defenders maximum advantage. There was no cover in what looked like fifteen hundred to two thousand yards of river bottom. Once he got out into the plowed, muddy fields, the Germans could pick him off because he couldn't move very quickly. All of what he saw meant the briefing was not going to be a picnic. He headed for the briefing with at least the knowledge of what they were up against.

On the way to the briefing, he flashed back to a ridiculous and absurd briefing he had attended in France prior to the attack on St, Lo.

At the briefing, the executive officer, a colonel, stepped forward and said, "Men, I want you to pay close attention. In case a man is wounded or it is necessary to get a message through, only one man will return to the rear. If there are four men on a mission, three of them must continue the mission while the other goes back. This applies to whatever may happen. Another thing, all vehicles will be at sixty-yard intervals. Anyone who violates this will be sent back and miss the fun."

He muttered to himself, "Is he crazy?"

The colonel conferred a moment with a general, and then turned to the men again and said, "It's been changed. One hundred yards is the interval, one hundred yards."

He had attended many absurd briefings when he was fighting in France back in the Spring. The most absurd was the insistence by the commanders that each company commander had to produce a quota of five German prisoners a week.

Colonel Bingham had a crude map and an aerial photograph spread out on an old wooden table in the bomb shelter in the paper mill. When he got to the briefing, Captains Kimbrough and Keys were just arriving. The map and photograph didn't look like they would be helpful. All four officers looked at the materials.

He said, "What the hell is that?" pointing to an obvious oval formation on the west side of the river.

"I dunno. Looks like a racetrack or something – some kind of stadium."

"Is it for horses or people?"

"I dunno."

Pointing to another feature he asked, "What is this?"

"Well everyone in headquarters thinks it's a swimming pool." The rectangular structure was several hundred yards north of the racetrack and overlooking the river.

"Whatever it is, we know that it is defended by machine guns."

"I don't see any installations around the racetrack."

"No. No activity has been observed there."

"Yeah, and these are tennis courts."

"Yeah, but no activity has been observed near the courts."

"What is in the trees south of what appears to be an athletic complex."

"We don't know," Bingham said.

Trees and underbrush covered all of the area south of the collection of athletic facilities, and he didn't like the way it looked. What bothered him the most was the high ground on the west side of the river. From his familiarity with topographical maps, he knew that rivers don't run through hills. They run around hills. This river ran through a hill. This meant that somebody had hauled a hellova lot of dirt to the west side of the river and piled it up. And, it hadn't been done recently because there were large trees growing on it. But it had been done with a lot of labor and a lot of motivation to create a formidable elevated fortification.

"Okay, the Germans have probably mined the roads so we are gonna send out three companies as soon as it gets dark.

Captain Shearer, you take your men and head for the farmhouse, the Nierstein *Gut*, and then on to the racetrack. Stay off the roads and out of the farm houses."

"Do we know if the *Gut* is occupied?"

"No. We don't know."

"Captain Keys, you take G Company and come in from the north of the racetrack."

"Okay."

"Captain Kimbrough, you take I Company and attack toward the Hasenfeld *Gut* and try to capture the swimming pool."

"Colonel, we're gonna be sitting ducks out there if the Germans catch us in these muddy fields if they are ready for us."

"I know, and we're under strength, but maybe at night, we can surprise them. We have got to know what the Germans have set up and where their defenses are located."

They all knew it was going to be a risky probe at under-strength, with the enemy having the advantage. No one said anything or needed to. They had done this before, and it was what was done when they didn't have any information about an enemy's strength. He had fifty, mostly replacements, men with no mortars or machine guns, and they were going to cross two thousand yards of muddy fields with no cover. In addition, the fields were probably mined. Most of the cities, up to this point, had been protected by fields of anti-tank and anti-personnel mines. If they hit the mines, the Germans would be directing fire at them instantly with their machine guns and mortars.

"Are we gonna get any artillery support prior to the attack?" he asked.

"No, we can't get them up here in time. And, if you run into trouble, you make the decision to pull back if you have to. We need to capture these objectives but we don't need to get everyone killed trying to do it."

"Yes sir, I'll get the hell outta there if it gets too bad."

"Also sir, I think we need to let headquarters know that there are 88 shells, crates of them, stacked all along the railroad tracks running north and south. It looks to me like the Germans were planning a major offensive before we overran them. It really looks like they had planned to kick the shit out of somebody to the south of here."

"I'll pass the information along. Headquarters should be interested in that information."

"Good luck tonight, and stay on that radio to let me know what's going on out there."

"I will. And, I'll bring you a fresh basket of sugar beets for breakfast."

"Also, before I forget, I'd like you to call back to Herleen and see if they could get us some dry socks and boots. We will probably need them after we get out of those muddy fields." He wanted to avoid the deadly trench foot, and he didn't know how long they would be in the fields.

"I'll see what I can do, Captain."

He hadn't known Colonel Bingham very well, but he seemed to be closer to the men, under his command, than other divisional commanders or "cadre" officers.

"Cadre" officers were full-time training officers who often acted superior to officers like himself who were not on a permanent training assignment. On several occasions, he had detected this status difference. It made him mad as hell when he tried to purchase in the post exchanges tri-color mechanical pencils for writing on maps. He had been told that the pencils were reserved for "cadre." And, it made him mad now to see that the troops in the field were still wearing leggings while the officers in the rear areas were wearing the new heavy leather combat boots with a buckle top around the ankle. Anyway, Colonel Bingham didn't seem to show an elitist attitude as much as some of the other divisional commanders, but he was wearing the new boots.

He left the briefing with the other company commanders and headed back to the railroad tracks with a foreboding, chilling, and slightly nauseous feeling. He didn't like the way things looked at all. He had been trained to keep his thoughts focused on the military objective and the welfare of his men, but his emotions of fear, anxiety, and dread frequently betrayed and overcame his training and tried to seep into his awareness. The Germans had a total strategic and tactical advantage. The mud he was picking up in his boots reminded him of what knee deep mud was like.

Soldiers can't run in deep mud. Shit, they can't even crawl very well in this!

He has been raised on a farm in Ohio and knew from experience how hard it was to maneuver in the sticky mess. Still, he knew he had to get the men ready and show a commanding attitude. He only hoped that he could get to the objective of the racetrack without losing too many men. And, if they got stuck out there, he told himself he wouldn't get them cut off and unable to return to the American lines or be rescued.

So, he figured the best way to approach the assignment was to "go like hell" to get there and if he had to, he would "go like hell" to get out.

When he got back to the embankment he walked to each group of foxholes and told the men they were leaving as soon as it got dark and to leave everything except their rifles, ammo belts, canteens, and shovels. He wanted them stripped down to only what they needed.

The heavy overcoats slowed them down already, and if they got wet and muddy, the extra equipment could add extra weight that could prove to be costly when they needed to move quickly.

"It's about a thousand yards to the farmhouse. There are probably Germans in it so we could catch hell about half way there. Spread out and stay off the roads and lanes. Don't return their fire. It will only let them know where we are. And, we may need the ammo later. Of course, if they come out after us, then on my command you can fire at them. Get some rest. We're leaving after it gets dark. That's all for now."

The rest of the day it drizzled while the fifty men stayed in the paper mill to stay dry.

"Private, you're gonna be my radio operator. Do you know how to operate a radio?"

"Yes sir, I was a radio operator in England."

"Good. You've got the job. Just be sure you stay with me at all times."

"Yes, sir. I sure will."

"You know how to shoot that thing?" he asked the private.

"Yes, sir! I sure can."

"Okay, I think you're gonna need to use it."

"Yes, sir. I'm from Oklahoma, and I've been shooting guns my whole life."

He couldn't see how the radio would be needed because there wasn't any possibility of support troops, air strikes, or artillery support. But, he didn't dare be without it because he might need to talk to the CP about his position and strategy.

The night came quickly and the dark figures began to move from their burrows like zombies from a freshly dug shallow grave.

He thought, *these are just kids, and I'm taking them into a hellish situation. We're just going out into these fields to see if the Germans will kill us. Cannon fodder!*

A word he remembered from combat infantry training school kept repeating in his head like an obsessive echo.

Dispensable! Dispensable! Dispensable! He could feel his hands starting to stiffen with some loss of feeling. He had felt the near-paralysis in his hands when he was fighting in France. He didn't want it to return.

Not now!

Chapter *Three*

The *Gut*

O N HIS COMMAND, THE FIFTY WARRIORS IN overcoats, rifles at port arms, and wet helmets glistening from the falling mist moved up, over, and down the east side of the railroad tracks and trudged toward the cluster of farm houses called the Nierstein *Gut*. They were now unprotected from enemy fire. He directed them to move slowly and spread out on a compass course of east-southeast. He told them to go slowly because every approach to a structure that the allies had previously encountered had been extensively mined. The tails of the long olive drab colored wool overcoats flapped in the dark as the drizzle and wind raced across the muddy fields in a steady sweep. The men wearing them were hell-bent for Valhalla.

The fields were not frozen yet, but he knew from the chill on his face that they would freeze during the night. It was early in the evening, about 7:00 p.m. They faced what ordinarily would be an easy march and a short way to go, but they knew the German guns could start shooting at them at any time. He placed two point men out in front of the group while he was positioned in the rear of the company. He could barely make out their ghostly shapes.

He was worried and concerned that they were so lightly armed for a frontal attack on German positions, but he was confident they would fight like banty roosters. He had seen young American soldiers fight in France so he wasn't worried about their fierceness, aggression, and tenacity.

"Tell the men to keep in voice contact, and use hand signals where they can," he said to each of the soldiers forward and to the right and left of him.

"Watch out for trip wires!" he said, knowing they couldn't see a damned thing in the dark.

He didn't want the men to get spread out too far and get disoriented in the dark. When he looked through the water dripping off his helmet, everything on the ground around him looked the same in all directions, a muddy plowed field. The foreground in his immediate view was gray, bleak, drab, and objectless. He kept blinking his eyes because the surroundings were playing tricks on his depth perception, peripheral vision, and spacial orientation. His plan was to try to get to the racetrack, or whatever the hell it was, during the night if they encountered no resistance. If they did receive fire, he was going to use the Gut for some protection, reconnaissance, and a reevaluation of the best way to get to the objective of the *Sportplatz*.

"Thump. Thump. Thump." The 88s across the river were sending shells whining, screaming, and racing over their heads toward Koslar and the paper mill. They could hear them exploding behind them as the flashes lit up the sky. It was the usual nightly shelling. Each flash would faintly reveal the company of men advancing in the muddy field.

The going was slow, deliberate, and with fits and starts. Mud was sticking to his boots, and each man had to stop periodically and try to reduce the extra weight clinging to their feet. He had them stop and stand quietly after what he judged was about a hundred yards. He wanted them to catch their breath, and he wanted to listen for the unmistakable mechanical sounds of mortars and machine guns being loaded and positioned.

He knew the guns would make telltale noises if they were being readied. He also wanted to listen for the whine of the engines and clanking of the metal tracks of an 88 mm self-propelled gun. All of the sounds of ordinance being readied were seared into his memory and awareness. The sounds frequently consumed his nightmares in the hospital.

He heard nothing, and he didn't see any lights in the direction they were heading. There was only the wind, darkness, and the occasional sucking sound of a boot being pulled out of the mud. He calculated they were five hundred yards from the *Gut.* There was still not any German fire. If the Germans were in the *Gut,* the next five hundred yards would be where he and his men would receive the fire from the deadly guns.

The gently sloping hill they had been descending had now become flat river bottom, and the mud and water were becoming deeper. One of the point men signaled for the group to stop and for him to move forward. When he got to the forward position, he saw what the point man had seen. He saw hay bales! There were four or five rectangular hay bales in the sugar beet field, lined up end to end.

"What?"

"What's going on?"

"What tha hell are they doing here?"

The point man had a blank look on his face that indicated he was nonplussed and didn't know the answer to the captain's rhetorical question. He had asked the rhetorical question because he knew there wasn't any hay being raised within a hundred miles of where the bales were laying. The disturbed mud and footprints behind the bales indicated that the bales had been brought in and used by the German defenders as forward observation posts. Furthermore, he didn't see any spent shell casings. There wasn't anybody here now. Still, he sensed the men in the company had increased their level of vigilance like animals sensing danger in the wind. He knew fear would do that to a soldier. The bales were proof that the Germans were obviously very close, and the company had been recently observed by the enemy's forward observers.

Damn, that means they're really close! They've been watching us and could have shot us anytime.

The company slowly moved again toward the *Gut,* and they were positioned about one hundred yards from the cluster of farmhouses.

"Aaaagahh!...... Thud!....... Splash!" He heard a commotion coming from the direction of one of the point men.

What tha hell was that? The Krauts surely heard all of that noise.

He moved up quickly to discover that one of the point men had fallen into an antitank trench in the dark. He was sprawled in the bottom of the partially flooded trench.

He's damned lucky the trench wasn't mined!

"Hit the dirt," he told the men.

He feared any Germans in the Gut were sure to have heard the commotion. The entire company was lying in the mud as the point man tried to recover from his unintentional and unceremonious dive into the watery repose.

"Let's go", he said. "Get your butts in the trench."

I hope the Krauts didn't plant any mines in this trench.

Trenches were typically lined with buried "bouncing betty" mines or *Schrapnellmines.* As soon as they were activated, they would spring out of the ground five or six feet, explode, and spray metal fragments into the air. The sharp metal fragments usually created wounds that were fatal.

The company of men jumped into the trench, slipping and splashing in the flooded bottom of the depression in the field. When he jumped in, he landed in about six inches of water in the bottom, but he knew the German machine guns wouldn't hit him and the others if they were in the trench because it provided a natural defilade. He immediately felt the bone-chilling water seeping into his boots. None of his men triggered a mine in the trench.

Whew! We beat the devil again!

Relieved, he splashed up and down the trench telling each man that they were going to make a run for the *Gut* in a few minutes.

"Pass it down! We're getting out of this ditch in a few minutes."

He added, "If you need to take a piss or a crap, this is the place to do it. Just be sure you move in the ditch away from the group." He didn't want to have to fall or jump back in the ditch full of feces if heavy enemy fire forced them back into the trench.

He knew that the German guns could let them have it as soon as they popped over the lip of the furrowed earthen protection. He gave the signal and the company, slipping and sliding, ran directly for the farmhouse. He fully expected to feel the thump of a bullet hitting his body any second. He had felt it before, so now the anticipation was intensely visceral. The dash seemed to him to be agonizingly slow. He knew these soldiers had run for miles in boot camp, but they didn't prepare for this quagmire. After the frantic dash, their bodies slammed against the brick wall of the farm buildings, making a series of thuds. There still wasn't a violent response by the Germans.

The cold wet air burned their throats and lungs as they gasped from the exertion of the long run across the sea of mud. They all immediately took a drink from their canteens and then leaned on their rifles.

They had barely stopped breathing heavily when they all heard the hell of exploding ordnance erupting and echoing across the fields several thousand yards to the north. They heard rifle fire, machine gun fire, and artillery bursts. The low-lying clouds reflected the muzzle flashes in one short flicker after another.

He thought to himself, *One of the other companies is in trouble at the Hasenfeld Gut, several hundred yards to the north. That means the Germans are ready for us, and we could catch hell also.*

The flashes and explosions in the distance continued. He ordered the company to search out the farm houses.

"Don't shoot any civilians!"

He paused and added, "Shoot all soldiers you find. We can't take any prisoners."

That order got their attention. Their eyes got wider and flashed back and forth as they looked at each other for verification of what they had just heard. Shooting at German soldiers at two hundred yards was one thing, but shooting them at point-blank range wasn't something they had anticipated.

He heard several comments when they moved away to search the rooms in the buildings.

"Hard-core."

"Hard-assed."

"Mossbacked."

He smiled after overhearing their descriptions, and he wasn't sure one of them wouldn't freeze or panic if they did see an enemy soldier. He hoped one of them wouldn't start shooting up the *Gut* in panic. He knew it could happen with replacement soldiers.

His order to them was prompted by his memory of a sad incident that happened in France back in the spring. He came upon a private under his command that was distraught, crying, and hysterical because he had shot and killed a French farmer.

Looking through a hedgerow, the soldier had seen a farmer leading a cow. He started receiving fire from a hedgerow across the field from his position. He said he accidently shot the farmer's cow when he returned fire.

"That's okay soldier. We see dead animals all the time."

"I know, but the farmer collapsed on the cow and started wailing and crying over the loss of his only cow."

"Yes."

"Well, I couldn't stand seeing him grieving over the cow so I shot him also!"

The private became more hysterical.

"I couldn't stand it, captain. I couldn't stand to see him cry."

The soldier continued to cry over the incident and say, "I'm so sorry. I'm so sorry." He didn't say anything else to the soldier. All he could do was walk away and return to command the rest of the men.

Company L searched the farm houses that consisted of three buildings with a ditch or small stream running between them. At first, they couldn't find an entrance in the brick wall around the Gut, but then found an opening in the wooden barn that led to the rest of the building.

He searched several rooms with his .45 un-holstered and ready. He flashed back to searching farmhouses in France, but this farmhouse was different.

This doesn't look like any farmhouse I've ever seen. It looks more like a bunker or fortification. I hope we don't find any dead bodies in this place.

It didn't take the soldiers long to determine the farmers, who had lived there, raised hogs.

There was the familiar smell of hogs and an even stronger smell of decaying hogs lying around the outside of the *Gut*.

As soon as they entered the *Gut* he said, "Watch out for booby traps. They're booby-trapping more now. They had plenty of time to rig'em before they left."

He added, "If you need to take a crap, use the privy outside. Just don't get yourself shot. Stay next to the wall." He knew the ultimate indignity for a soldier was to be wounded while he was taking a crap. He was also slightly annoyed that he was having to give orders to the men that would have been normally been given by lieutenants or sergeants.

"Captain, the basement is full of mines and it looks like the Germans have been storing them for use at a later time."

"Mines?"

"Yea, the basement's full of un-detonated mines."

"Well, maybe they didn't have time to lay them out for our reception party."

"Yea. That's too bad," one of the men said sarcastically while the others grinned through their mud covered faces that showed below the brim of their helmets.

He guessed the Germans didn't have time to move them back as they retreated. Or, they couldn't get them across the muddy fields. What he couldn't figure out is why they hadn't just detonated them.

Well, they've got plenty more. They're probably out in the fields.

He now had a decision to make concerning whether to stay and dig in at the *Gut* or press on to the objective of the racetrack. It was after midnight and it had taken longer than he hoped to get to the *Gut* and secure positions that could serve as a jumping-off point for the next expanse of beet fields. It was also below freezing, and he wanted to see the terrain in the daylight before going any further. But, it meant spending the rest of the night and the next day stuck at the *Gut*. He radioed back that they were digging in and had encountered no resistance. He just couldn't figure out why the *Gut* wasn't defended. But, in the back of his mind, he knew the enemy could start shelling the farmhouse at any time. They knew the distance to the farmhouse. Consequently, it was an easy target, and they weren't likely to miss it. He knew the guns would be pre-set. If that happened, he feared he would have a hard time preventing his panicky soldiers from scattering from hell to breakfast.

He told the company to dig in and they would attack the next night. All night the battle raged north of L Company at the Hasenfeld *Gut*. They saw the flash of exploding artillery and the flicker of a burning tank. The attack to the north had obviously run into heavy resistance. The next day, the company got a closer look at the farmhouses, and he got a better look at the five hundred yards between them and the racetrack.

The farmhouse was not like the houses he had searched in France. According to 29th Division orders, troops were supposed to stay out of houses and barns, but the order was never followed. German soldiers could be hiding in the house and storage facilities, and he didn't want to get surprised and shot from behind by a sniper. So, this house wasn't spared inspection by L Company either. They looked for booby traps and didn't find any, thankfully. Fortunately, they also didn't find any German soldiers or civilians hiding in the house or any spent shell casings.

The soldiers found jelly, pickles, and canned fruit in the cellar where the mines were stored. They looked for a chicken to cook or eggs to eat but didn't find any. They found clothing lying around the farm house as well. Shoes and socks had been strewn about. They found some ammunition clips, a cartridge belt, and a German helmet. The helmet wasn't a German combat helmet. It was painted black, lighter in weight, and appeared to be a fire or civil defense helmet. Nevertheless, it had swastikas on it. The German soldiers had been in the house and taken a mattress off one of the beds. There were pictures strewn about of family members who had served in the First World War. The walls were adorned with religious pictures, crucifixes, and family portraits. No one had lived in the house for some time, so it was dank and musty from the rains of the last few months. It looked like to him the farm house and store rooms were several hundred years old. The bathroom facilities were still in an outhouse outside, and the water came from a well or cistern. The storerooms were mostly empty but had contained the sugar beets that were grown in the Roer River bottoms. From the looks of the muddy earth around the house and muddy tracks in the house, there had been a lot of activity at the *Gut* prior to the arrival of L Company.

The company dug in along and adjacent to the protected walls of the Gut and waited for dawn. They cleaned their weapons that had gotten muddy during the night, smoked, and ate parts of the C-rations they had stuffed in their wool shirt pockets or pants pockets. He told them they would leave about the same time as the night before.

The next day it was again raining, and he wanted to get a good look at the five hundred yards they were going to have to cross after dark. He went around the *Gut* to find an observation position that would let him survey the background with his field glasses. The falling rain and fog rising from the river and fields made the visibility very poor. He couldn't see much in the distance, but he was determined to be in position if the weather briefly cleared. He heard the thump of mortars as they went up and watched the smoke barrage that was being prepared to blind the enemy for further attacks on the Hasenfeld *Gut*. He could tell there was a helluva fight going on for the farmhouses that were north of the swimming pool.

For a brief period of about thirty minutes right before 12:00 p.m., the clouds cleared. He scanned from left to right and couldn't see anything beyond the tree line. The trees and residual fall foliage obscured everything from the far left to the far right of his view. He knew there were structures beyond the tree line somewhere in a general direction, but he didn't get any specific information or clarification about what lay ahead. What he saw mostly was a flat, drab, lifeless, objectless, monochromatic, and unremarkable landscape a hundred and eighty degrees from right to left.

They would just keep going until they could find cover. The five hundred yards they were going to cross looked truly like "no

mans land." The potential German positions were well above
the river plain, perhaps thirty to fifty feet. The enemy, without
question, had the advantage. They had the elevation: They could
see him, but he couldn't see them: They were protected: He wasn't.
In addition, he and his men had lost their mobility in the mud. They
couldn't move right or left, advance, or retreat quickly to avoid
enemy fire. For the German gunners, it would be as easy as shooting
fence posts like he had done many times in Texas before the war.

He had to get fifty men across the open field before they
reached any cover or protection from German fire. Unequivocally,
the situation looked very bad and tantamount to a suicide mission.

The rest of the day he tried to get some rest. He periodically
moved among the men in the company encouraging them to
keep their weapons out of the mud. And, he stressed to them to
not shoot at ghost or phantom German soldiers. He knew that
long hours of looking down range could play tricks on a person's
perception so that they began to see things that weren't there.
Objects in the distance could begin to take the form of enemy
soldiers. These were untested soldiers, and he didn't want them to
be "trigger happy' and shoot at imaginary targets, waste valuable
ammunition, and reveal their positions. He didn't want to get to the
racetrack and not have any ammunition. That would be curtains for
them.

When he was out of the rain and alone he smoked his pipe,
took the pictures of Skip out of his billfold, and looked at them
for several minutes. They were minutes he cherished and looked
forward to.

Most of the soldiers in his company rested and tried to get
some sleep. He let some of them rotate into the *Gut* and out of
the rain. The German guns hadn't shelled the farm complex yet,
so he took the risk of letting them stay dry in shifts. They found
relatively comfortable diverse spots in the *Gut* to snooze and smoke
cigarettes.

As usual, there were conversations between the resting soldiers.
He overheard some of the chatter.

One of the soldiers who had been in combat asked, "How long is this mission going to last?"

Another answered, "I reckon a few days. Shit, who knows?"

"I wonder if I'll live through it?" another commented without any gloom, anxiety, or fear. He seemed to be only speculating in a matter of fact way like wondering if it was going to rain tomorrow.

They all had trained with the Garands, carbines, and Browning Automatic Rifles (BAR), and they knew how and what to do with them. He also knew that firing these weapons was different when someone was firing back. Unfortunately, mud reduced the weapons to near ineffectiveness. All of the weapons could get clogged with mud. The barrels and chambers got clogged. The gun stocks got muddy and slippery. The clips and magazines, caked with mud, made loading the weapons very difficult. Sometimes the weapons had to be loaded one round at a time. He thought that maybe he should have kept going last night instead of waiting at the Gut. Still, no one had been killed yet, and the comfort of that fact was offset by the apprehension, fear, and uncertainty of the very next step because if they entered a mine field, the next step could be the last, individually and collectively.

In his gut, he knew the mines were there. The German Army wasn't stupid. They knew military tactics. That's where he would have put them. Based on all of his combat training and experience, the placement of the mines made sense tactically and strategically. They knew that an advancing force would have to cross the five hundred yards of open ground. It was a concealed shrapnel trap and he was going to spring it.

Hopefully, it won't be a coup de grace!

He was especially apprehensive because he had done this before in France at St. Clair and at Villers-Fossard when he went back to get three wounded men who had been left behind when his company withdrew a short distance. The German fire had been heavy in these situations, but at least in France, there was some cover of the hedgerows for protection. Here, if the German gunners detected their advance, it would be like "shooting ducks on a pond." The German forces waiting on the high ground could pull the triggers on the powerful machine guns and launch the deadly mortar rounds. He also learned that if a soldier got wounded, he would likely have to get himself back to an aid station.

Images flashed across his mind of the many men in France who died from a lack of medical help. Some were killed instantly, but others sustained major and minor wounds. In either case, they bled to death where they lay. He had been lucky. He didn't bleed to death.

The images of combat back in the Spring of 1944 were fresh, vivid, and seared in his mind. He tended to ruminate about the experiences in France after the invasion whenever he had idle time. That was what was happening while he was sitting and waiting to make his attack on the *Sportplatz*. His present reality was inextricably connected to previous combat experiences. This time, however, he knew all too well what it was like to be under fire from the enemy.

The images from the battle for St. Lo stayed with him for a very long time. Thirty years later, his former executive officer, Major Charles R. Cawthon wrote an article that was published in *American Heritage*. He read and responded to the article.

Route 2 Box 447
Terrell, Texas
June 17, 1974

Mr. Oliver Jensen, Editor
American Heritage
1221 Avenue of the Americas
New York, New York 10020

Dear Mr. Jensen:

We just received the June issue of American Heritage and read with a good deal of interest Charles Cawthon's article on the attack on St. Lo in July 1944.

I commanded H Company, 2nd Battalion, 116 Regiment, 29th Infantry Division under Major Cawthon at that time and would like to expand on his remarks. On page 10, he mentions receiving replacements at St. Clair-sur-l'Elle. I was in that group and took command of H Company that night. On pager 11 he mentions a staff officer being killed over his head. That officer was Lieutenant Charles Talbot of Massachusetts who was assisting houses and barns. The cottage was actually a stone smoke house, and when we arrived in the small building, there was a freshly cut smoked ham and a German mess kit on the table, indicating that the previous occupants left in a hurry. Lt. Talbot went up a ladder on the outside wall into the loft. He yelled to me to hand him a rifle because he saw an enemy soldier beyond a hedgerow. I handed him my rifle and in a minute or so he was killed by a hail of bullets from our own troops.

On page 82 Mr. Cawthon mentions mortar and machine gun ammunition being short due to the storm on the beach. Actually, we were allotted three 81 mm mortar shells per gun per day and 250 rounds of 30 caliber machine gun ammunition. He also mentions having eight machine guns. If my memory serves me right, we only had three guns and one of those had a bullet hole in the water jacket. We were supposed to have six 81 mm mortars, but only had three and one of those did not have a base plate.

The major took quite a kidding on the shrapnel in his face because the two wounds, one on each side, were exactly where dimples were supposed to be.

On page 85 he mentions the casualties on the first morning of the attack. I was one of those company officers that were hit within thirty minutes of the beginning of the attack.

I am including with this letter a picture that I am sure Major Cawthon does not know exists since it was developed by an X-ray technician in the hospital after I was wounded and evacuated. The prints were not made until I returned to the states much later in the war. It shows the officers of H Company on the burned out German car opposite the Battalion Command Post mentioned on page 82. Front left is Lt. Shepard, Co.O. 1st section of mortars. This officer from Minnesota was killed by the same German that wounded me and my radio operator during the attack on St. Lo a few days later. Next is Lt. Raggett, who was killed later at Vire. Lt. Harvey was C.O. of the 1st Section of Machine Guns, Lt. Woodworth was C.O. of 3rd Platoon. On the left on top of the burned out car is myself, Lt. Noble from West Virginia, C. O. of 2nd Section of Mortars, and Capt. Murphy from Canton, Ohio, was the Executive officer of H Company.

I hope that you will find these comments interesting, and if you would be so kind as to forward this letter and pictures to Charles Cawthon, he will find them of interest.

Please send me three additional copies of your June issue. If you have Charles Cawthon's address, I would appreciate having it.

Respectfully yours,
Robert L. Shearer
Capt. Inf. Rtd.
Terrell, Texas

This time in battle he knew the realities of the carnage created by artillery, mortar, rifle, and machine-gun fire. The sights, sounds, and smells were suppressed and stored just below his level of consciousness. All of his memories had plagued him in the hospital when, uninvited, they came back to him from time to time.

Nevertheless, he now steeled himself to protect and save as many of his men as he could come hell or high water.

That's it! No more beating around the bush. Let's get tha hell outta here!

Chapter Four

The Attack

THE DRIZZLE CONTINUED, AND DARKNESS settled over the *Gut*. After rousing the sleeping soldiers who desperately wanted a few more seconds out of the rain, the company formed and began to move along the brick wall of the *Gut*. He told the men to spread out and keep a distance between them, but stay within hearing distance. He didn't want a mortar barrage to take out several men at one time. When they left the *Gut*, he knew the mortars shells could hit at any time.

He couldn't see anything in the distance, but he had taken a compass reading when the weather was clearer. He planned for them to stay on a northeast course. On that course, he hoped they would make contact with the racetrack. He knew they had about five hundred yards to travel before they would find any protection beyond the flat open terrain.

He told the radio operator to send a message they were on their way. He had set up a three-man point with a corporal in the lead. When they started, there wasn't any fire from the Germans. He told the company to stop and rest after two hundred yards. He still couldn't get a mental picture of anything in the dark. They sloshed across small ditches full of water that crossed the fields parallel to the river. He hoped the ditches might offer some protection if the German guns opened up on them.

What tha hell! It's all the cover there is in this muddy field.

Crossing the muddy sugar beet fields was slow, disorienting, and exhausting.

He thought to himself, *If the Germans can't see the company, they damn sure can hear us.*

The men made sloshing and sucking noises as they pulled each foot from the calf-deep mud. He was having trouble making progress because every time he stepped down, he didn't know how far down his foot would go because of the depth of the mud. Some steps took him knee-deep and others were only inches deep. So, the short rest for the men was welcomed. He guessed they were a little over two hundred yards from the line of trees. He motioned for the radio operator and BAR man to stay close to him.

He had always preferred to be close to the BAR man since the spring offensive in France. The BAR had tremendous firepower, and it was the only automatic weapon they had. Unfortunately, it used a lot of ammunition that someone had to carry.

They began to move forward again, and he could barely see the outline of the tree line in the distance.

Still no German fire! It was completely dark now. He couldn't see the oval but he knew exactly the direction to move to reach it.

He said to the radio man next to him,

"We're sitting ducks…"

"Click!"

"Whaaaaam!"

After the flash of the explosion, the sound echoed across the muddy field.

"Damn!"

The flash and explosion came from the direction of one of the point men. The mine had popped-up and exploded five feet in the air. He knew one of the point men had tripped a wire and been hit by the mine. All of the soldiers froze in place, terrified to take another step.

"Click!"

"Whaaaaam!"

They saw the flash of light and heard the sound of another mine explode.

"Hit the deck," he called down the line of men. The entire

company of men flopped face down in the mud. He knew they were less likely to be hit a piece of shrapnel if they were prone instead of standing.

"Pop!"

"Pop!"

"Pop!"

Three aerial flares, fired from somewhere beyond the trees, rose in the overcast sky and illuminated the field around them.

"I'm hit!...Aaagh…uhhhhhhh."

He and the rest of the men were face down in the deep mud, and he felt the cold water seeping in along his waistline and sleeves.

"Whump. Whump. Whump."

He heard mortars belch their deadly explosive missals in the distance. He knew the sound well.

"Pop. Pop. Pop."

More flares rose in the air and flashed above them.

"Zzzzzzthump. Zzzzzzzthump. Zzzzzzzzthump."

Damn! I knew it. I knew it! I knew it! M 42! M 42!

He heard the unmistakable sound of several German M 42 machine guns firing continuously from the woods south of the racetrack. He knew the sound well, as well as the muzzle reports of all of the German field weapons. The M 42s fired twice the number of rounds per minute as the American machine guns. They fired so fast that a single shot couldn't be discerned from all of the others. The sound he had heard before was like the sound of a buzz saw. The M 42s could keep them pinned down forever because the suppressive fire was so intense and unrelenting.

Tracers whizzed at them from several points. Mortar shells exploded all around him with yellow flashes of light. Simultaneously, machine gun bullets hit the mud all around him.

"Splat. Splat. Splat. Splat." Sugar beets, water, and mud filled the air and covered him and the men near him that he could see. The sounds of the mortars exploding and machine guns raking the company blended into a deafening roar as the

German defensive positions poured the deadly fusillade of

explosive and deafening ordnance on them.

More men screamed that they had been hit. Some had dived into the water-filled depressions and hit mines that had been planted there. The rest just lay motionless in the field.

He yelled at his orderly next to him to see if he was okay and to make sure he stayed down. He was okay. He knew sometimes soldiers panicked, bolted, and ran helter-skelter in the confusion and intense noise.

"Splat. Splat. Whump. Whump. Whump. Thump. Thump. Thump."

Mud flew through the air and landed everywhere.

An all steel and lead hell was breaking loose now, directly on them. More mines exploded. Mortar shells were exploding. The bullets from machine gun fire were churning up the muddy field and hitting the men.

"Oh shit! Oh shit! We're pinned down," he heard a voice behind him say.

He yelled to the company, "Stay put! Don't move!" He didn't have to worry about the Germans hearing him because of all the noise and, besides they knew exactly where the company was located in the field.

"Zzzzzzzzthump. Zzzzzzzzzthump. Zzzzzzzzthump. The arcing path of machine gun fire from the trees kept on coming. He could tell the Germans were hitting them with two hundred and fifty round bursts so that they didn't overheat the barrels on their guns.

"What the hell is in the woods?" he said out loud.

"Whump. Whump. Whump." More mortars raced and arced high through the air toward them coming from the direction of the oval.

The shelling continued for what seemed like hours and then he heard an unmistakable sound. The muzzle blast and sound came from the racetrack. He knew, even above the other explosions, that it was the report of an 88 mm self-propelled gun. Then he heard the familiar whining sound overhead when the rounds hit somewhere behind them.

"Swoosh. Whaaaaaang."

No one could rise up. He clawed the mud and tried to cover up.

The radio man yelled to him, "We're catching hell, captain." The German guns had them trapped, and they were pinned down and getting ripped up. He knew several men had to be dead or wounded.

"Whump. Whump. Whump."

"Crack. Crack. Crack, Crack…Crack."

He heard rifles firing. No one could move. He couldn't see anything in the dark but mud when the shells exploded around him. He could hear wounded men moaning, screaming, and yelling. He knew it was important for the young soldiers to keep hearing his voice so he kept yelling as loud as he could to stay in communication with the men. They could panic and leave their positions. They would start asking themselves if he was still alive and if they were the only ones still alive.

He kept yelling, "Stay down! Hold your fire!"

In the middle of the barrage, a private panicked. He rose to his feet and started running in circles. The first machine gun bullet splintered the stock on his Garand. Then in rapid succession, bullets hit him in the left shoulder, left thigh, and chest. He didn't seem to go down but staggered around in the muddy field.

Go down! For God's sake, go down!

It seemed to him like the killing was happening in slow motion and took forever for the young soldier to finally flop in the muddy field.

He put his head down on his muddy arm and said to himself, *Poor bastard panicked.*

The intense fire lasted about twenty minutes. Then it became slower but steadier.

A few mortars were launched, and staccato intervals of machine gun fire continued. He waited to see if he could hear the Germans changing the barrels on the machine guns, which he knew they would have to do. He didn't hear anything. The 88s stopped. He told the orderly to call down the line and find out who'd been hit. He could hear the voices calling names across the pitch black, muddy field. Several didn't answer.

The orderly replied after a minute or so, "So far, captain we've got seven hit, some wounded, some no answer."

"Call back to the command post in the mill and tell them we're pinned down and have lost at least seven. Ask them if they have any good ideas," he told the radio operator.

"They said *no* captain."

"Okay, tell them I'm going to wait for daylight and resume the attack the next night."

He guessed the German gunners wouldn't expose their positions during daylight unless the company started moving again. They knew he couldn't move in the daylight without taking heavy casualties. So he and his men lay in the mud the rest of the night.

The thought of spending the night was bad enough, but another day would be miserable. The choices were not very good.

At least I could get a bearing on the tree line, he thought. He was close enough to see it very well, but he knew the German defenders were going to reload the guns and pour it on them again as soon as it got dark.

As the time approached midnight, it began to get very cold. The ground was freezing except where he was lying. The wetness was slowly seeping through the wool clothes. He was covered in mud. He reached down to his pistol belt to make sure he still had his .45s. He did.

He told the orderly to tell the men to stay put and check for mines and trip wires around the area where they were lying. He told them to watch out for the small ditches full of water. He told them to get their weapons ready because German infantry could be advancing on their positions at any time. Most of the men still had their Garand bayonets that they could use to probe around to make sure they weren't laying next to a mine. As an officer, he didn't have one, but the orderly who did have one cleared a safe distance around where they were lying. He told the orderly to pass the message along that each man needed to clear a path in front of them.

He knew they would be making a dash the next evening and he

wanted to lose as few men as possible to the insidious mines before they reached the objective. His hope was that they had gotten well into the field of mines and close to being through and clear of it before they started their dash across the field the next evening.

The lethal and grisly truth would emerge immediately if they continued to hit the mines for a long distance between where they were and the objective of the oval. If that happened, the few men that survived would either be captured or killed.

The mud made their weapons useless if it blocked the end of the barrels or got into the chambers of the rifles. It was almost impossible to keep the mud out of the clips because the men and weapons were covered in mud.

Some of the wounded men could be heard moaning not very far from the lucky ones who were still alive.

"Help meee! Help meee! I'm over here! Help me!" he heard and then he would hear a moan. The helpless, stranded, and wounded men would periodically make moans all night.

He said to his orderly, "Poor bastards. Nobody can help them." He couldn't get water or medical attention to them because of the threat of a mine.

His hands and feet were getting very cold now and it was raining harder. He knew it was going to be a long day in the sugar beet field but hopefully, the German shelling would subside.

Daylight came slowly because of the lingering fog and the steam rising from the river to the east. He immediately recognized the company wasn't spread out as badly as he had imagined. He figured they'd be spread from hell-to-breakfast across the field. They had sustained several casualties in the minefield.

He knew some of his men had been killed or wounded, but he had lost fewer than he expected. Some of the prone figures weren't moving, and the mud was pink around them. He knew they were dead.

He wanted to move among the men to support and reassure them because he knew the first experience of combat was frightening for the seventeen-year-old soldiers. They had to be scared because he was scared to death. He couldn't approach any of them because of the buried mines. All he could do was pass commands along to them to sit tight and be ready. He knew that there was some comfort and security for them knowing the company commander was still alive. It could reduce their level of fear and anxiety.

When the sky got lighter, he began to make out the shape of the oval about three hundred yards in the distance and beyond the tree line. He could also see the line of trees south of the oval and to his right.

He wondered, *What is in the trees? That's where most of the heavy fire had come from. It has to be a major gun emplacement.*

He could see through the mud-covered field glasses that the racetrack had an embankment around it, at least on the side he was looking at. A brick wall, four to six feet high, stood on the crest of the embankment. He immediately recognized that if he could get the company to the embankment and dig in, it would be harder for the German guns to target and hit them.

It looks a damn site safer than where we are.

It looked to him like an oval was built protruding into the river plain with very little rise on the uphill side. Just at the edge of the trees stood a large brick building where some of the fire had come from.

He thought, *Well, son….. of….. a…… bitch! What the hell is that building?* Aerial recon hadn't indicated anything except German soldiers in the swimming pool. But that was A Company's problem. He had been told that nothing had been seen in the oval during the daytime, but he was sure the mortars, that had kicked their ass the night before, had come from the direction of the oval.

It must be a pillbox or bunker.

"Okay corporal, pass the word along that we will be moving out at dusk."

All he had under his command was privates and one corporal, no sergeants or officers. He told his radio man that they were damn sure gonna get to that embankment and dig in like hell.

"Radio back to the command post that we are moving out at nightfall."

He added, "Tell that BAR man to stick close to us, and tell the company I want all weapons loaded and in working order."

During the day it was cloudy and light rain fell. He couldn't withdraw if he had wanted to because the Germans could see every move they made. All of the men lay in the field with only a slight rise in the terrain for protection from a possible storm of machine gun bullets.

His mind flashed back to the cold and rain in Louisiana at Fort Polk while he was on maneuvers. Those were miserable times in his life. But, this was unimaginable because the weather was similar, but here any move could trigger a mine. Besides, no one was shooting at him in Louisiana. The troops burned pine stumps to keep warm. As a result, they all got covered with black pine soot which made them stink to high heaven.

The filth and smell got so bad that he had gone AWOL when he secretly went into town to take a bath and clean up. Thank God the army didn't find out about the little excursion. His infraction didn't seem so important now as he lay in a frozen, wet field on the German border. But, the heat from one of those burning pine stumps would feel good right now.

Lying in a muddy field all day gave him a lot of time to think. His thoughts returned to swimming in the spring-fed pool of Vickery Park north of where the family lived in Dallas and swimming in the Colorado River when they lived in Bastrop while he was stationed at Camp Swift. He also kept thinking about the hospital in England. It had been very bad for him, emotionally. The hospitals in England were very depressing because he had seen the hundreds of wounded, burned, maimed, and dying young boys on a daily basis. The young soldiers were depressed because they didn't want to go home disfigured or crippled.

They cried a lot and moaned from the pain. Many died in the hospitals. On his wards, many were severely psychologically disturbed. He didn't see how they could make it back home. He also wondered about what the effect would be on himself.

He thought about how he had wanted to be a career army officer after he completed ROTC. But he didn't get the active duty commission because of the goddamn physical. He thought, at the time, his military career was finished. If he had gotten an active duty commission, he would be at least a colonel who rarely got out of the command post. Hell, he might even have one of those shitty little dogs the generals all seemed to keep with them at all times. His military career was finished until the bombing of Pearl Harbor.

Who could have seen that coming? He was a civilian and reserve officer. Look where I am now. I'm commanding a bunch of seventeen-and eighteen-year-old kids, most of whom were replacements. Most of the lieutenants had been killed at the battle of Koslar or one of the battles leading up to this one.

And, I've got half a company, no machine guns, no mortars, and I was trained to command a heavy weapons company. Now, I've got less than fifty kids with rifles and one BAR. I don't know any of them and I don't want to.

He had learned fighting in France that it was better to not know anybody or make any friends. It just made death harder when it came if you knew them. Unfortunately, he had known some of his lieutenants in France. Most of the intelligent, strong, and young junior officers were dead.

He could feel the emotions rising and he couldn't make himself not think about the faces and names of Lieutenant Pankow, Lieutenant Raggett, Lieutenant Shepard,

Lieutenant Talbot, and his orderly, Private Eugene Shearer. And, he was only in France for four weeks. They were all gone, and he was still here in this flooded muddy field.

Why? Am I lucky? When will my luck run out? he thought. The situation in the field looked to him to be close to his luck running out.

He could feel his emotions welling up, and he knew he had to get control and get back to the situation at hand. It wouldn't be good for his troops to see him crying right before an attack. He was all they had for leadership. He could be the difference between them living or dying. He never thought when he had a nervous breakdown in the hospital that he would ever get back in this situation. But, the cold and wet ground next to his overcoat made it easy to switch to the reality of the trap he was in now.

"Pass the word down the line to anyone who can move out

when I give the command. We're gonna run like hell for the cover of the embankment. Don't fire your weapon. It will only draw more fire. When you get to the embankment, dig in," he said to the orderly.

The order was passed among the muddy figures. He knew they were ready to get out of the muddy and wet plowed field, so they probably wouldn't have any trouble kicking into high gear running across the field. He also knew they were scared to stay and scared to move forward. He was correct in his assumption. Consequently, it didn't take them long to resolve their avoidance-avoidance conflict.

They were still in the middle of the minefield, so he knew some might not make it out. He hoped that enough men would make it to make a stand and fight once they could get some cover.

We came to fight and by-damned we're going to do it!

Three hundred yards in the open is a long way to run under fire, much less in the mud. But, they had all been trained to achieve an objective, so no one complained or questioned the order. At least if they cussed, he didn't hear it. He knew they couldn't stay where they were.

Nightfall came and he told the men to get ready.

"Okay let's go."

At different times, over forty men got up and started running though the mud. When he got up, he could tell the wool overcoat was very heavy from being soaked in water.

"Click…wham!"

Another mine exploded. One of the men to his far right didn't make it two steps.

"Click…Wham!"

Another mine exploded. Now the Germans knew they were there and on the move once again. They opened up with machine guns sweeping the muddy fields as they had done the previous night. Their dash was noisy, sloppy, frantic and agonizingly slow.

"Thump…Thump…Thump."

Mortars were landing behind them. This was a lucky break, but he knew they would either walk the impact zone forward or backward.

Hopefully, the mortars will stay behind us, he thought.

After about twenty-five yards, he could tell he wasn't in as good a shape as when he went into St. Clair after months of training. He was really breathing heavily. At least they weren't in full pack, but the company made a lot of noise splashing through the mud and water. He kept looking to his left and then to his right while he ran toward the objective.

"Zzzzzzzzzthump! Zzzzzzzzthump! Zzzzzzzzzthump!" Machine guns, spitting fire and steel, opened up on them from the direction of the trees. The rounds were hitting all around him. After about fifty yards, the soldier to the left and slightly in front of him slumped forward went down.

Hell, I'm watching men die and I don't even know their names. The poor bastard never had a chance, he said to himself.

"Click…Wham!" Another mine exploded off to his right.

"Zzzzzzzzzzthump…Zzzzzzzzzthump…Zzzzzzzzzthump." The machine gun fire never let up. He ran for several yards and didn't hear any more mines exploding.

We must be through the minefield.

"I'm really starting to get winded," he whispered to himself between gasping breaths.

Go! Go! Go!

At two hundred yards the machine gun fire let up and seemed to be coming in behind the company. He had hoped the angle of the fire would help them, and it was looking like the German gunners couldn't hit them because of the degree of the angle.

He hoped like hell that was the case.

He was really getting winded. His legs were beginning to feel like rubber. His throat was burning from the freezing air. He could feel his legs becoming uncoordinated so that he was really getting wobbly.

With only a few yards to go, he could make out the shadow of the embankment. He couldn't run as fast as he wanted to, and he was sweating his clothes wet under the wool clothing. He and the others crashed through the tree line and headed for the embankment.

The earth of the embankment was hard as he fell against it. Other soldiers collapsed around him, making a lot of noise. His orderly landed right behind him.

What was his name? Jensen? Jansen? he asked himself.

What tough bastards these guys are, he thought to himself. They were all breathing heavily and gasping for air. They took their canteens out of their canvass covers when the men finally had a welcomed chance to wet their dry throats after breathing the burningly cold air.

"Damn!" He looked at his canteen, and water had sloshed all over him because the black bakelite lid had been shot off, and the lip of the metal canteen was mangled. He still managed to get a drink, but it was a sobering reminder of how close the machine gun bullet had come to his body.

Then it got very quiet. All he could hear was the men breathing heavily. It stayed quiet for about fifteen minutes, and then he heard German voices coming from the other side of the embankment.

He guessed they couldn't be more than twenty or thirty feet away, as the crow flies.

"Bump!...Thump! Thump! Thump!"

A stick grenade called a "potato masher," landed on the embankment next to him and bounced down the embankment and flew end over end beyond him into the field. He turned away from the grenade.

"Wham!" The grenade exploded and he felt small metal fragments hitting his wool overcoat and helmet.

"Shit!"

"Get your butts up and move higher on the embankment so the grenades will roll to the bottom," he yelled to the company.

He wasn't worried about the Germans hearing him because they obviously knew where he was.

"Bump!...Thump! Thump! Thump!"

"Wham!"

"Pass it along to dig like your life depended on it," he said to the orderly.

Shovels came out, and he could hear the digging going on.

Okay, now I can move around and see who made it and check with the ones who did.

The embankment, while hard-packed and slippery, wasn't as muddy as the field had been. He knew they were somewhere on the south end of the oval. The embankment and the wall on top weren't very high, but the curvature was only slight, so it was larger in circumference than anyone at the command post had figured. And he knew for sure the German soldiers were only a few feet away on the other side. They were still making a lot of noise. They heard voices and machine guns being loaded. Overriding all of the sounds was the occasional high pitched whine of an engine and the clanking of metal tracks. He knew that meant a tank or self-propelled gun was on the other side of the oval some distance away.

These were the sounds that got his attention, raised his level of fear, and changed his strategy because the company of riflemen was no match for heavy guns.

These are heavy weapons, but thank God they're not right on the other side of us.

As he started crawling and walking stooped over on the earthen bank like a goat on the side of a hill. he thought, *At least we're out of that goddamned muddy field.* But, it was still dark and still raining lightly. And, he was still soaked, still cold as hell, and still in peril.

When he moved to his right, checking with each man, he told them to watch out for the grenades bouncing over the top.

"If it doesn't roll down the hill, throw it back over," he said. He had seen soldiers in Normandy do this before with the "potato masher" when the Germans threw the grenades over the hedgerows. The new replacements, by the look on their faces, thought he was nuts. It was a risky thing to do because he had also seen soldiers get their arms blown off trying to throw the grenades back or away from themselves a safe distance like Lieutenant Harris did on the morning of the attack on St. Lo.

The last man down the line was perched high on the embankment that overlooked the curvature of the oval. It was barely discernable in the dark, but he could see the embankment curve faded into the dark.

"What have you seen, private?"

"Nothing, sir. But I can see a little way around the hill."

"I can hear them captain," he said.

"Yeah, I've heard them too."

"Sit tight. I'm going to send some help your way."

He went back to where he originally flopped against the bank and where the orderly and radioman were. He wanted to see how each man was doing in the dark protection of the embankment.

"Okay, I'm going to the left to see who is with us and what our total strength is," he said to them.

He crawled to the left passing each man in the dark.

"Hi, captain."

"You okay soldier?" He noticed that the private didn't look over seventeen years old.

"Yeah, but McCracken over there is hurt pretty bad. Shrapnel in the thigh, I think."

"Private, you okay?"

"Yeah, I've got a bandage on it. I'll be okay. I've been hit with shrapnel before."

He could tell the private had lost some blood and was experiencing some symptoms of shock.

"Do what you can, and I'll get you some more bandages to change," he said to him.

To the left and right on the embankment, he checked all of the rest of the men and had some bandages passed along to the wounded private. He counted thirty-eight total and one who was wounded. The mine field had been lethal.

"Thump! Thump!" A grenade landed by Private Hosek but didn't roll down the hill. The Germans had made a mistake because Hosek had been in France in the spring. He picked up the potato masher and heaved it back over the wall. With a flash and loud bang, it exploded in the air over the other side of the brick wall. He hoped that by the time the Germans let the grenades count down longer, the men would be dug in, and only a direct hit on a foxhole would be deadly.

As he moved back to the right, he counted twenty men and told each of them to move further to his right along the embankment of the oval. He wanted eighteen men positioned to his left and twenty men to his right.

Okay. Okay, we're here! One at a time they spread out and dug in. He could hear some grumbling from being annoyed at having to start digging again. The twenty men slipped and groped one at a time through the dark and positioned themselves against the bank along the curvature of the structure.

No response came from the German guns.

"Corporal, you're in charge of the group in your direction, so stay close so I can let you know what we're going to do next."

He didn't have a plan, but he desperately wanted to see the layout of the place in the daytime. He had twenty men spread out along the embankment to his right and eighteen, in addition to himself, to his left. The German soldiers were still making a lot of noise in the dark on the other side, but no counterattack came. Ten minutes went by.

He saw a flash of light then heard, "Whaaaaaam!" The massive sound roared through the dark. He woke up after a few seconds with his helmet slammed against his head and bricks and mortar scattered on top of him and the ground around him.

He saw another flash of light and heard the sound again.

"Whaaaaaam!" The massive explosion shook the ground and a blanket of bricks and mortar covered the men.

"The goddamned Germans are blasting the top of the brick wall with 88 mm artillery shells," he yelled to his orderly.

"They're probably coming from a self-propelled gun on the higher ground on the other side of the oval," he said.

"Tell the men to stay dug in."

He crawled to the left and right and reassured the men that they were protected from being hit. But, he knew the 88 had a way of psychologically disorienting a soldier, because the concussion could knock you unconscious, and the sound was deafening to the point of losing your hearing. He had seen troops killed in buildings in Normandy on the first floor when an 88 hit the second floor or roof. They had been killed by a massive concussion, so the vicious shrapnel wasn't all the damage a big artillery shell could do.

"Whaaaaaaaam!"

Another 88 hit the top of the wall above their heads, but further down the line, and bricks and mortar rained down on their positions.

He told himself he had to get to the men to his right so he worked his way along the foxholes in the embankment until he got to them. He couldn't see anything. He yelled across to the first solder and told him he was coming. He moved along the line and checked on the twenty men. And then he worked his way back.

It was getting late, after midnight. There was no sign of the Germans, just a lot of activity and sounds. He heard voices, clanging, and banging sounds.

What tha hell are they doing over there?

"Pa-pop! Pa-pop! Pa-pop!" There was a pause and he knew it was rifles firing.

"Tat! Tat! Tat!"

Shooting erupted off to his right around the curve of the oval. The night lit up like the light from an enormous bonfire. He immediately ran bent over toward the action.

"Pop! Pop! Pop!.......Pop!..............Pop!"

He heard more rifles firing.

"Swooooosh!"

The flame thrower roared and came toward him and the eight or nine men closest to him.

"Swooooosh!"

The wall of flame seemed to be washing over them. The gunfire intensified.

FmW 41! FmW 41!

Several MP 40 submachine guns intensified their fire and the 9 mm slugs hit all around them.

Several soldiers yelled,

MP 40!

MP 40!
MP 40!
He thought, *Schmeisser!*

He was familiar with the *Maschinenpistole*. It fired a 9 mm cartridge. The American troops called it a *Schmeisser*. He was also familiar with the *Flammenwerfer 41,* the German flame thrower or FmW 41. He had seen them lying in the ditches along the hedgerows in France, abandoned by the retreating German Army. He knew the flamethrower fired in ten-second bursts of gasoline mixed with tar and burning oil.

Now, the German attackers were shooting through the flames. He yelled at the men to get back and hit the dirt. More small arms fire came through the flames.

"Iiiieeeeeeeee," he heard someone scream. More rifles fired. The area to his right erupted in massive white and orange flames. The whole side of the embankment was burning with the jellied gasoline.

"Pop! Pop!...Pop! Pop! Pop!"...He heard bursts of submachine guns being fired.

"Tat! Tat! Tat!" The guns were pinning them down. His men were returning the fire but they couldn't see who to shoot at. A private crawled up to him who had come from his right.

"Captain, they're chewing us up. We've been returning fire but we can't see."

"How many hit?"

"I dunno, maybe five or six. The guy to my right got hit. He was about fifteen yards to my right. I don't know what happened to the rest." The flame throwers kept coming and spitting their burning jelly.

"Whooooooosh!" A flamethrower lit up the sky behind him. He heard more shooting.

"Hit the dirt private. They're behind us also. Return fire but don't waste any ammo. We may need it later."

The two of them crawled forward with bullets passing over their heads.

"Let's get to the next foxhole," he said.

He wanted to locate his orderly and the radioman. He also wanted to get to the BAR man.

They waited for the Germans to do something. It seemed that after thirty minutes, the attack had ended. He crawled, once again, toward his right. The smell of the burning fuel was overwhelming. His throat and nostrils burned from inhaling the acrid smoke from the flames.

He found the first man because he could see the flames from the jellied gasoline still flickering on the man's body. The stench of the fuel burning flesh and wet wool was the worst he had ever smelled. He fought back nausea. The soldier had been off to his right and the Germans had surprised him and burned and shot the poor bastard at almost point blank range. He found four more flickering black corpses. They had died and had never seen the attackers. He worked his way further along the embankment and called into the darkness.

"Corporal?" He heard nothing.

"Corporal, give me a report." He heard nothing. He waited. No voices responded.

"Corporal?"

"Captain, this is Private Neal," a voice said from the dark area where the fight had occurred.

"The corporal is dead."

The private was crying and hysterical. He could hear him thrashing around the other side.

"Oh God! Oh God! What's happening?"

"How many hit?"

"Uh,......Uh,.......Uh,......Three. Four. Five. No wounded. I don't know. I can't see anything in the dark. They ambushed us sir, on us before we knew it. I think we've got fifteen left, maybe more."

"Okay Private, wait thirty minutes and if there's no more action, you and the rest of you get your butts back this way. Bring all the canteens, ammo, and weapons. Also, bring any bandages."

"Okay, sir."

He heard the private hysterically and frantically scrambling around in the dark, and he knew he had to get them all together again. He got in the foxhole along the bank and pointed his radio man's M1 rifle toward the darkness as the men got ready to come his way.

The men came along the slippery bank one-by-one. The Germans had them covered with a machine gun and when they heard the commotion they started firing.

"Zzzzzzzpop! Zzzzzzzpop! Zzzzzzzpop!...Zzzzzzzpo! Zzzzzzzpop!"

"Damn," he said to himself out loud, "They're close."

He quickly shouldered the Garand and returned fire directly at the muzzle flash of the machine gun. He saw the first two men make it. He was firing rapid fire now with clips pinging as they flew out of the chamber. He kept jamming the M1 clips in the chamber and firing at the muzzle flashes of the MP 40 submachine gun. With each shot, the recoil of the rifle slammed against his shoulder like he was used to because he had fired the battle rifle many times. He saw the third man go down on the muddy bank.

He kept pulling clips out of his ammo belt just as three more men made it back to safety.

The barrel of the Garand was white hot from the rapid fire. The barrel was steaming when the drizzle hit the hot metal. The MP 40 submachine gun didn't let up. He saw another man go down. He knew the rest were too scared to rise up, but they were more scared to be left alone if the company pulled back. So they kept running and scrambling along the embankment.

He had used up a lot of ammo, but fifteen men made it back. They pulled back to the main group and found any hole they could get into.

He thought, *Shit, that was a big mistake to get twenty men cut-off.* Now the company was down to thirty and as far as he could tell they hadn't killed one German soldier. He knew he had to get them regrouped and figure out what to do next.

"Whooosh! Sssssssssssssssss!"

He heard the hiss of the flame thrower and then the roar of

exploding fuel. The night was lighting up like an orange jack-o'-lantern.

"Taat! Taat! Taat!...Taat! Taat!"

The Germans were attacking again. This time, the company was ready. The thirty men spread out up and down the embankment and started firing at the flame thrower.

"Get that BAR into position and give em' hell," he yelled at the group of men during the hellish fog, frenzy, and vortex of battle.

All of his men were firing their Garands, reloading, and spitting out empty clips. The BAR was sending a steady stream of fire at the flames. The fight lasted a few minutes, and then the flames stopped, the shooting stopped, and everything was instantly dark again.

It was quiet and he tried to adjust his eyes to the sudden pitch darkness. He smelled the burning fuel. He heard noises coming from his right.

What's going on? What? What's next?

He waited. The men made no noises, and he knew they had to be numb and in shock after the firefight.

"Okay, give me a count."

They were all together so he could hear each name. After the names were reported, he could still count thirty. No one had been hit this time.

"Okay, everybody dig in. It will be light in a couple of hours, but they might come back."

He knew the Germans would be back. The enemy had them trapped. They knew it and he knew it. He didn't know what he was going to do next, but he was determined to keep thirty men alive.

"Whooooooooosh."

This time, the flame thrower was behind them. Again they fired their rifles.

"Pop! Pop! Pop!"

The Germans were attacking behind them. This time, the men were dug in and could protect themselves and return fire.

The flamethrower lit up the embankment again as the German

soldiers fired from behind the protection of the flames. This time, the attack only lasted for about twenty minutes. But, it was clear that the enemy was north and south of the small group huddled and trapped on the racetrack embankment. If they went over the top, they would be shot instantly. If they tried to leave across the muddy field, German soldiers could shoot all of them before they could get fifty yards.

Son of a bitch, we're boxed in!

Again, dawn came slowly because of the fog and steam rising from the river to the east, not far from where they were. The thirty men looked like unrecognizable creatures that had just burrowed out of the underworld. They were one color, grayish mud. They had mud covered faces, uniforms, and helmets.

He could only see the whites of their eyes darting around in the heads of the mud creatures. Worse, they were all exhausted, cold, and wet. They were lying in foxholes in the embankment like fetuses. Some were eating the small amount of food they had managed to stuff in the pockets of their field jackets and overcoats before they had left the railroad tracks two days ago. They could see the bodies of their dead comrades lying in irregular positions on the slope of the racetrack. From the smell, he could tell some of the men had peed or shit in their pants.

He could hear the soldiers mumble, "Poor bastards."

"I'm going up to the top to see what's going on," he said to the orderly.

"You protect that radio he's got over there 'cause it may be what keeps us from getting our asses kicked any worse."

"Don't worry captain."

He paused and added, "I wouldn't stick my head up too far over the edge if I were you."

"I'm sure not going to."

He crawled to the top of the wall and took off his helmet and raised it slightly over the top with his hand so that the crown of the helmet was slightly exposed on the other side. No one shot at him, so he looked over the edge. He didn't see any enemy soldiers. He put the helmet back on and readied his field glasses and focused them over the edge.

He still saw nothing. He didn't see any German soldiers anywhere. Then his thoughts started racing as he put it all together.

They're coming in at night from across the river in the city. There's no one here in the daytime because they would be exposed to attack from the air. Before the recent overcast, there had been several attacks on the area.

Then he looked at the details of the oval, trying to take in the whole picture of the place. There was a sloped dirt track. It was a very large oval with no seats and no running track. The sloped dirt track was steep starting at the base of the wall and dropping sharply to the grassy field.

He immediately recognized foxholes and gun emplacements that pitted the surface of the track. He could see them and the expanse of the oval track without the field glasses. It was obvious to him the banked track was used for races of some kind.

Through the field glasses, he could see to the left, beyond the low stadium and the tennis courts, a two-story building that must have been a swimming pool with a metal catwalk over the top of the pool. He noticed a diving tower. He guessed the German soldiers were still entrenched there like air reconnaissance had indicated several days ago. When he looked through the field glasses, he couldn't see any Germans, but he could see evidence in the disturbed fields of a lot of recent activity. What disturbed him the most were the waffle-like indentions of track marks in the dirt and grass left by heavy vehicles. He knew they were made by tanks and self-propelled guns with metal tracks.

The main center part of the oval looked like it contained four playing fields, but he could see they were larger than football fields, and there were no goal posts. He then put it all together.

It's a goddamned soccer field. This is a soccer stadium, but there aren't any seats. He had never played soccer before, but this sure looked to him like what soccer fields should look like. Except for the tank tracks, the grassy fields were undisturbed.

So, he figured this had to be a complete sporting or athletic complex, but it was the longest oval track he had ever seen.

He hadn't mused about what he had seen very long before a structure to his right immediately got his attention. He raised his field glasses again and looked through them. To his right, and on the edge of the wooded area was a brick and concrete blockhouse that had never been mentioned in the briefing. It showed signs of three aerial pock mark hits, without sustaining much damage. It had small doors and no windows.

What the hell is that thing? he questioned. It wasn't a bunker. It was too old and it didn't have any firing ports or slits. It was just a brick building about a story and a half high. He also saw well-worn paths leading from the soccer stadium to the mysterious building.

He suspected there were German soldiers inside the building with machine guns because some of the intense fire he received in the beet field had come from the direction of the blockhouse. The tracers had pinpointed its location. But it was located such that it wasn't positioned for them to train the guns on the embankment where he and his men were located. And, there were thick trees and underbrush between them and the blockhouse.

Even so, the sight of it gave him a few chills, because the company had no equipment that would allow them to approach the fortress. It would take a tank, heavy artillery fire, or a very heavy aerial bombardment to neutralize the building.

He slid back down the embankment to join the orderly.

"What did you see Captain?"

"Nothing. No Germans,"

"What?"

"That's right. Not a German in sight, but they've been here."

"It looks like they come across the river at night, and after they've given us a welcome party, they go back. But, they still have machine guns pointed at the fields from the swimming pool and that goddamned brick fort off to the right."

"What is it?"

"I don't know. But, it's not gonna be easily knocked out, not by us that's for damn sure. This whole area is heavily fortified. I guess that's what we were supposed to find out."

As he sat on the wet embankment, he knew it was time for him to figure out what to do.

I'm up against insurmountable odds of survival! We don't stand a Chinaman's chance of capturing any of these fortifications.

He sat and looked at the muddy beet fields, their tracks leading back to the Gut, and the grey drizzle coming down on them. If they were ever gonna get back alive through the field, they had to go that night because the safe paths back through the field would eventually be washed away unless if started raining harder. If it rained harder, the tracks would be gone in an hour or less.

He was sure the enemy would be back during the coming night and they would be more prepared to attack the company. He guessed they would hit his few remaining men very hard if they got another chance. He hated the thought of getting on the radio to tell the command post he was pulling back. He hated the idea of retreating. It grated on his military training standards, personal aggressiveness, and combat staunchness.

Everything in his training and preparation focused on realizing his objective. He had also seen in France what could happen when soldiers get cut-off, isolated, and trapped. They're likely goners. And, he couldn't trust there would be a second American attack anytime soon to free them if they got trapped.

So, he weighed the options as he looked out at the godforsaken muddy sugar beet field. If they returned in the safe tracks, they might not lose anyone. If they stayed where they were, all were likely to get killed or captured, and he didn't see any hope of holding on to the one-fourth of the oval he held.

"Click. Click. Click."

"Captain!"

He whirled around and saw standing on top of the brick wall a diminutive, unarmed German soldier with his hands in the air in broad drizzling daylight. Several of the men in the company had flicked off the safeties on their rifles when they saw him. They had pivoted in their positions in order to point their rifles at him from their new positions. They had their fingers tight on the triggers of their rifles. They didn't relax or let go either.

The soldier looked to be about thirteen years old. He was

wearing a helmet that was far too big for him…like a little kid playing army with his friends.

"Hold your fire! Hold your fire," he said loudly.

The soldier had an "X" in white paint splashed across the front of his oversized wool tunic.

What tha hell? Is this kid surrendering?

No one said anything for a second or two, and because they were so surprised, they just froze in place and stared at the kid. They could have killed him in a flash. He was surprised but glad none of the young soldiers shot the kid. The German soldier looked very frightened as drops of rain ran off his helmet from all sides.

"You must surrender or be killed," he said in English with an obvious German accent.

He thought briefly about surrendering, and then an image flashed through his mind about the quality of the food in a concentration camp. He also thought about Skip and the boys and the warm weather in Texas.

I think I'd rather fight my way out of here and not lose these men that trust me. I'm not going to be a goddamned prisoner!

"Tell your commander I said go to hell", he yelled at the young frightened soldier.

The toy-like soldier stepped back curtly and disappeared.

Several of his men made comments:

"Damn, what was that?"

"Well, I'll be a son of a bitch!"

"That scared the pee outta me!"

"Where the hell did he come from captain?"

"Hell if I know."

The men were dumbstruck, nonplussed, and looking at each other like they had seen a doppelganger. The German soldier had been right in front of them. They had seen many dead soldiers, but this one was alive and very close, even if he wasn't armed.

He thought, *Shit! That was really odd. The Germans don't take prisoners. I've heard many rumors, going back to the time of the invasion, of them shooting prisoners. And, an army in retreat doesn't take prisoners…slows them down too much. I'm sure about that. That was nuts, completely nuts.*

When he looked at the men and they looked back, he could tell the surrender demand accomplished one thing. It brought a company of fatigued soldiers back to a state of complete vigilance. He didn't know whether they were shocked or scared, but they damned sure were awake, vigilant, and functioning at a higher level of combat readiness.

Let's see if we can get our butts outta here!

Chapter Five

The Withdrawal

THAT NIGHT HE DIDN'T GET MUCH SLEEP. THE decision of what to do next kept him awake most of what was usually a fitful night of sleep. The decision created a deep inner conflict. He hated the idea of running like a frightened rat, but he was trapped physically and psychologically. In his mind, he tried to sort out all of the dichotomies that ate at his gut. The conflict was painful, wrenching, and deep. His thoughts oscillated between the choices: fight or retreat; give up or fight on; run or kill the enemy; save the men or attack; live or die, and stay put or go back. It was the most painful decision he ever had to make, and the thought of failing made him angry, sullen, and irritable.

Damn! Damn! Damn!

"Get me the CP on the radio," he said to his radio operator.

"I've got to figure out what to do by the time it gets dark."

A voice came on the other end of the line.

"This is Captain Shearer. Is this Colonel Bingham?"

The leadership in the command post may have changed recently, so he wasn't sure who was in charge.

"This is Bingham."

"We're pulling back tonight," he told the colonel, but it galled him to have to tell him.

"What's the situation out there?"

"I've lost twenty men…got thirty left. The Germans have us pinned down. If we stay here, they're gonna finish us off. We can't hold the objective."

"What are they throwing at you?"

"Eighty-eights…mortars…flame throwers…machine guns… small arms…and mines in the field. The machine guns are in the pool and in the blockhouse in the trees. They bring in the 88s at night."

He added, "It's gonna take a helluva lot more than what we've got to knock out these defenses. We couldn't do it in a month of Sundays."

"Get your butt back here the best way possible. Wish we had some cover fire for you. Good luck….Captain." Colonel Bingham knew the American casualties in the assault across the Rhineland had already been extensive. He knew he didn't want the loss of an entire company to add to the mounting losses.

We've got to get our butts outta here PDQ! Damn! Damn!

Additionally, his anger was starting to well up into his consciousness. He was angry because he knew he and his men should never have been sent to attack the German defenses with such a light force. The anger was compounded by the anger brought with him from his previous time in combat. He had managed to keep the anger in his subconscious so he could effectively lead his men. But, after this insane mission, it was starting to affect his emotional control.

In addition, he had an innate sense of needing to accomplish something that meant something. Or, he needed to something that had meaning, even if was only a small accomplishment or something where the meaning wasn't totally clear or only partially understood. Specifically, he needed for his efforts and the loss of his men to count for something in the war effort. He wrestled with meaninglessness. Watching the waste of the lives of young soldiers killed in combat caused him to have deep feelings of angst, anger, and anomie.

The question he repeatedly asked himself was, *What is an acceptable loss of men in completing a successful mission? Are there no limits in the slaughter?* He couldn't answer the question, and divisional command didn't seem to have a sense of acceptable losses in relation to an objective. If fact, they avoided the subject.

What he had heard from divisional command was:

"You have to advance," and

"You have to make the enemy know you'll keep coming," and

"We must be ready to meet anything," and

"You must prepare yourself for anything the enemy may throw at you," and

"Be on alert. Be on guard."

Finally, "We are going to carry this mission out."

Without guidance from divisional command, he felt detached and alienated from the overall direction of the missions he had been given. When that happened, he suppressed his feelings, became numb on the surface, and extremely angry at a subconscious level. The reservoir of anger kept building up the longer he spent in the front line. Based on his experiences, the emotional equation invariably precipitates emotional difficulties in the future, depending on the severity, duration, and buffering of the suppressed anger.

It would be the last time he would ever talk to Colonel Bingham. But, the colonel did survive the war and went on to have an excellent and decorated career after the war.

He sent word to the thirty men that they were pulling back at dusk. They seemed to be relieved they wouldn't have to face the flamethrowers again. If he waited any longer, the muddy path back through the lurking, leaping, and lethal mines would be washed away by the rain, and the Germans could attack anytime.

I hope like hell it doesn't start raining hard.

He told the men that they were going to go back in the muddy tracks that the company had made, initially, advancing across the field. He figured if one of the men didn't hit a mine, the Germans wouldn't know the company had left the embankment of the oval. He knew the Germans would come after them with greater strength, firepower, aggression, and manpower than the night before any time they wanted to.

"Get the mud out of your weapons and get some rest before we get the hell out of here."

The men looked too exhausted to do anything, much less slug and plod across fifteen hundred yards of muddy field. They hadn't eaten. They hadn't slept much, and the cold and rain was taking its toll on their energy reserves. But, he knew that if they didn't have the benefit of those safe tracks through the field, there wasn't much hope for them. The path was their way to escape the battlefield trap they were in.

He was determined to get them back, and he planned to push and shove every damn one of them back to the railroad tracks if it killed him. He didn't think he could stand losing another man. He was sure he didn't want to surrender or be captured. He had to concentrate on the withdrawal, or he knew he would get very emotional.

Get 'em back! Get 'em back!

The boot tracks could be plainly seen in the muddy sugar beet field. Single file was the way they had to go, but he hated the idea. One mortar round or mine could take out several men in a single file formation. But, if they spread out, they would hit new mines and alert the Germans gunners again. After weighing the risks, he decided they would walk single file and head for the *Gut*.

He sent the order down the line and put a private from Kansas, who wasn't a very tall man, as point man. Who else could do it? His only corporal was killed the night before. He and his orderly would be in the rear of the muddy bunch as they sloshed back across the field to the *Gut*.

He also positioned the BAR man right in front of the two of them but also bringing up the rear, like they were, in case the German soldiers decided to follow them. He didn't think they would follow, but he knew they knew where the mines were located so he had to be cautious. He wasn't worried this time about one of his soldiers running the other way, but he was worried again about being close to the BAR man because snipers were fond of identifying and shooting the soldier manning the automatic weapon.

The light began to fade and it soon got dark. It was still drizzling. The muddy forms crawled from their foxholes and walked bent over, their muddy overcoats dragging in the mud, and their rifles slung over their shoulders. They formed at a point at the bottom of the embankment and started one-by-one across the muddy field. All he could hear was the sound of each boot being sucked from the mud with each step. The sounds seemed very loud to him, and he didn't see how the Germans couldn't hear all of the sounds of the reluctant and slightly ignominious escape.

They knew exactly where the mines would be waiting. The location was two hundred yards out in the field. The eyes of the men were nervously blinking and darting left to right in the dark cloudy night as they got nearer to the gauntlet of the deadly minefield. Each man knew a wrong step could be their last. They would step into a deep mud hole and sink down and then the next step hit a harder slippery spot. When they hit the shallow spot in the field, they lost their footing. Their feet would go out from under them, and they would land sprawled in the mud and water, grunting, cussing, and spitting out mud and water.

The column moved slowly and laboriously through the minefield. The pleading and doomed voices were faint at first but as they got close, they got louder.

"Help me. Help me. I'm over here."

There was a pause and then he heard, "Medic!...medic!...medic!" There was another pause and then the faint voices faded away.

The voices started again.

"Mamma! Mamma! Mamma!

The wounded men left from the first trip called out in the dark when they heard the company slogging through the mud. Moans and wails were coming from several locations. The wounded young soldiers were alive but, they were slowly dying where they lay. They were helplessly bleeding to death in a muddy sugar beet field in Germany.

The men in the retreating company, who normally would have tried to save them, were too exhausted to help even if they had wanted to. He started to tear and weep when he heard the agonizing and desperate cries for help. Their pleading tore and tugged at his emotional strength. He couldn't stand the sounds because he had heard so many men moaning from pain or crying because they were maimed for life. His memory of the sounds and sights in the hospital had brought on bouts of depression and had caused him to lose his emotional control on several occasions.

Thank God it's dark and the men can't see me.

With every labored step forward, the column slowly escaped the minefield. No one had tripped a mine yet. He felt relieved and passed the word up the line of men to go faster now. He was exhausted, relieved, and determined if only his body wouldn't fail him now. He tried to steel himself to muster more strength.

"Splush!"

He heard the first soldier collapse in the mud.

"Get him up, get him to his feet," he said with a loud whisper.

"Two of you get him up."

Two of the soldiers picked up the fallen man and dragged him between them.

A second man staggered and collapsed in a heap.

"You men up there get him up."

Two men got him up.

He knew why they were falling because he felt that he could go down any minute.

All of his strength was gone and he was straining to stay upright.

"I've got to keep going," he said aloud. Then his orderly slumped forward but he grabbed him and straightened him up. The appearance of a dark silhouetted form of a building ahead meant they were getting close to the *Gut* and gave them a slight burst of new energy.

"Keep going. Get all of the men to the *Gut* and we will rest," he shouted up the line. He shouted as loud as he could because he didn't give a damn now if the Germans heard him.

One after another, the men crashed and fell forward next to the brick wall of the *Gut* and out of line of small arms and machine gun fire of the enemy. They were all breathing heavily. They took the Garands off their shoulders and leaned them against the wall of the *Gut*. They were all hoping they wouldn't need them anytime soon. He knew the men needed rest, but the German gunners were sure to have discovered, by now, they had left.

They are gonna blow the hell out of this farm house complex. We can't stay here! They can easily target us! There wasn't much water left in the canteens, so he told the men to get a drink and leave the canteens and shovels but keep their ammo belts.

The muzzle report of the first 88 cracked from the direction of the oval. A shell whined across the field and fell short of the *Gut* and exploded.

"Wham!"

Another cracked, whined across the field, and exploded.
"Wham!"

"They're shelling the *Gut*. We've got to get out of here", he yelled at the pile of muddy human forms. He and the orderly crawled from man to man and told them that they must get to the railroad embankment. Most of the men had passed out from exhaustion. He grabbed the overcoat of a private who seemed to be in better condition than the others.

"Come on private. You're gonna help me get these men on their feet." The 88s were still firing and exploding, but they weren't hitting near them.

"Wham!.......Wham!.............Wham!"

They managed to get all thirty men up and moving again slowly towards towards the railroad embankment. About twenty yards from the embankment the clouds parted and a full moon exposed the group of retreaters like it was daylight.

His men had been silent until they reached the *Gut*. Now they were starting to chatter and curse again.

He could hear them exclaiming, "Oh God, I can't make it!"

Another said, "I can't go any further. I'm pooped."

He also heard one say, "I'm going down."

He thought, *What tha hell, the Krauts know where we are anyway so it won't make any difference if they hear my men talking.*

"Wheeang!" He heard the deadly piercing wail of an 88 shell passing overhead and very close.

"Wham!"

"Wheeang!" Another shell passed over them.

"Wham!"

The German gunners had seen them and they had the 88s pointed right at them.

I knew it! I knew it! It's only a matter of a short time before they adjusted their sights to put the high-velocity shells directly on us. We're sitting ducks.

"Get your butts over that embankment," he yelled this time.

"Go! Go! Go!"

"Wheeang…Wheeang."

"Wham-boom!............Wham-boom!" The sound of the shells exploding close to them echoed across the muddy fields.

The screaming shells were hitting in the mud on the other side of the embankment with tremendous explosions one after another. He reeled from the concussion of the exploding 88 shells. Several of the men fell against the exposed side of the embankment and couldn't make it up and over. The blasts were sending mud, water, and debris into the air. As they were ducking and running, the dislodged and ejected mess was splattering on the men when it fell from the air above their heads.

"Wham-boom!"

"You men over there pull these men over the top. Nobody gets left on this side."

They desperately and doggedly dragged the men up the embankment and over the tracks, and each group fell and rolled down the other side into a ditch filled with water. The men were grunting, cursing, yelling, and gasping for air in their attempt to get over the embankment.

"Get your asses over the hill!" he heard several of the men yell.

"Gawddamnit, get going!"

"Oh shit! Oh shit! Oh sh…………..!"

Groups of three or four dragged a soldier over the top and left slick trails in the mud where they had been. The 88 explosions struck fear, panic, and desperation in the soldiers that were still able to move on their own.

He and the orderly were the last to get to the embankment.

"Wheeang!"

"Wham-boom!" Another 88 hit and exploded on the field

behind them and the shock and concussion knocked them down, but they were luckily out of shrapnel range.

"Ugh."

He hit the ground with a thud, and the concussion and the fall almost knocked the air from his lungs. When he hit the ground, he landed on his left arm and could tell from the wincing pain that he had wrenched it when he fell. But, he managed to get back on his feet. He didn't know it, but he lost one of his .45s in the fall. It was dislodged from the holster and fell in the mud.

More men were being pushed and dragged up the railroad embankment in a disordered panic.

"Wheeang!"

"Wham-boom!" An 88 hit the embankment about twenty yards to the left.

"Wheeang!"

"Wham-boom!" Another overhead missile landed and exploded beyond the embankment.

He realized he had lost most of his hearing, but he could see the 88 shells exploding all around like a silent movie and feel the concussion from the shock waves. He staggered, but regained his balance. He got to the rails and saw the thirty men lying in the ditch which was partially full of water. Some had collapsed face down in the water.

Some of their rifles were submerged, and others were pointing in various directions.

"Get those men's faces out of the water or they will drown," he yelled down to the men flopped in the mud and water in various twisted positions, face up and face down.

Two soldiers stepped over the rails, and the soldier that was holding both of them up caught his boot on the rail, stumbled, and lost his footing and balance. They both pitched forward, head over heels. They landed in the water at the bottom of the embankment. Their rifles flew through the air, pin-wheeling end to end. Both rifles stuck, barrels first, in the mud.

He bent over and started side-stepping down the embankment

to get the men out of trouble. He stood in the ditch looking at the grotesque pile of men and made sure that their heads were out of the water. He was relieved he had gotten them back to safety, but he was passing in and out of consciousness and on the verge of collapse from total exhaustion.

He took one step forward, and he saw a sudden flash of light. He felt pressure on his whole back side. The 88 shell hit and exploded on the top of the embankment, directly on the rails. His body was thrown about twenty–five feet past where the thirty men were laying. The blast of the exploding 88 shell slammed his helmet against his head and knocked him down into the mud. He and some of the other soldiers were unconscious from the concussion of the exploding shell. They were below the lethal zone of flying shrapnel because of the height of the embankment, but the blast from the exploding shell was right above their heads. Being that close to an 88 blast had killed many other soldiers in the war.

The blast wave from the exploding high-velocity shell created an intense over-pressurization impulse on his body. It pushed on all of the organs in his body, especially air-filled organs such as his ears, lungs, and gastrointestinal tract. The over-pressurization wave also pushed on the fluid-filled cavities of his brain and spinal cord.

After the initial blast wave, he experienced an extreme drop in pressure, creating a vacuum from blast under-pressure. The blast winds reversed as the atmospheric pressure dropped. The extreme pressure differences on his body resulted in stress to his body when organs and tissues of different densities were accelerated or decelerated at different rates, resulting in his body being damaged by stretching and shearing forces.

He was close enough to the blast to suffer a concussion, traumatic brain injury, or a subdural hematoma. The blast could also have caused him to experience blast lung, eye rupture, and abdominal hemorrhaging. Wearing a helmet, no doubt, reduced the concussion symptoms and possible injuries to his ears, including perforation of the tympanic membrane.

Finally, he could likely develop neuropsychiatric symptoms as a result of the traumatic brain injury. Depending on how close he was to the blast, he could eventually experience headaches, fatigue, poor concentration, lethargy, depression, anxiety, and insomnia. The symptoms of his concussion could likely be confused with the symptoms of post-traumatic stress disorder. The symptoms could be a result of the concussion, post-traumatic stress from his combat experiences prior to the blast, or an interactive effect from a combination of the two disorders.

Whatever the case and eventual outcome, four factors were indicated about his condition after the 88 blast. First, his condition was very serious, complex, and precarious considering the extent of his injuries, his close proximity to the blast, and the level of his current battlefield medical care. Second, very little was known about the neuropsychiatric symptoms of traumatic brain injury. Consequently, any treatment he received for his condition would not consist of clinical procedures that were based on sound scientific evidence. Third, he would likely suffer from both short and long term effects of the blast. Fourth, a full recovery was likely to be a long and, perhaps, lifetime challenge. Nevertheless, he would not likely be the same after the war, depending on the extent of his injuries, his social, family, spiritual, and medical support at home. With all of his support at home, his psychological resiliency would also be a major factor in his recovery.

Chapter Six

Fini la Guere

THE TWO MEDICS IN THE AID STATION IN KOSLAR were looking over the wounded soldiers in the room full of men lying on army cots in the aid station. The two wounded soldiers brought in a couple of days earlier occupied their conversation.

"When did these two come in?"

"Morning before last, or the morning before that. I'm not sure."

"God, they look like hell…and I've seen a lot of bad cases."

"What outfit?"

"I can't tell. They've been covered in mud since they arrived."

"I think they're both from the 29th. I think one's a private and the other may be a captain or a major."

"No shit! An officer with rank?"

"Yeah, I checked and he was wearing two forty-fives, but he's only got one now."

"We don't see that much rank come through here. Where tha hell did he come from?"

"I dunno, but he hasn't been sitting behind a desk pushing a pencil that's for sure. And, he isn't one of those ninety-day wonders."

"This is a crazy damn war."

"Yeah!"

"He's been unconscious for several days."

"The medics who brought him in on the hood of a jeep said he should be dead as close as the 88 had hit to him."

"I checked him. He's got a good pulse, and he's breathing."

"Has he got his dog tags?"

"Yeah. I checked."

He paused and added, "He doesn't have any visible wounds, but he's out cold."

"Yeah, it looks like the 88 knocked the shit out of him."

"They also said there were a lot of KIAs (Killed in Action) where they came from."

"What tha hell, we had three DOAs last week and four the week before."

"Yeah!"

"Jeez, they said in England we were winning this war, but it damn sure doesn't look like it from where we are."

"Yeah, the replacements don't last very long in this miserable place."

"What tha hell, we just take 'em in, patch 'em up, and ship 'em out."

"You're right, it's a crazy gawdamned war, that's what it is."

"The private is conscious, but he's been burned pretty badly. Looks like a Jerry flame thrower got him."

"Anything else?"

"Yeah, he's also been hit in the leg."

"Looks like it."

"Yeah, he was brought in on one of those wooden beet carts like a lot of others."

"He got any German souvenirs on him?"

"Nah, he's clean."

What none of them knew was that, while the thirty men and the captain were laying on the safer side of the railroad tracks, the 29th was already making a second attack over the same fields the ill-fated company had just exited.

In the afternoon of December 6, planes attacked the *Sportplatz*. Artillery positioned around Koslar, fired eight-inch shells at the sporting complex that had been converted to fortifications. The attack concentrated on the facilities of the *Sportplatz*, especially the above ground swimming pool. The voices of the wounded men were again heard in the muddy fields as the next attack advanced.

Medics who had been brought up for the second attack found the company that had briefly taken the south end of the stadium. Medics were scarce and not frequently seen because the advance across Belgium and Holland had been so rapid. The units had outrun most of the support units and replacement medics. Plus, many medics had been KIA.

The main aid station in Koslar was a large stone building on a corner of the main street through town. Wounded men from the attack were brought to this location. The building contained many glass windows and looked out of place with the traditional old and somewhat drab buildings found in small towns in the area.

"These two are going out on a truck to Herleen as soon as the officer comes around."

"How long will that be?"

"Shit, I dunno. I've seen 'em out for a week before."

"All we can do is to try to get them out of here and on their way to the battalion hospital in Liege. They'll clean 'em up in Liege."

"They don't look strong enough to go anywhere. They're dehydrated, emaciated, and weak, and maybe they've got some frostbite or trench foot."

"Yeah. But they'll get better...................... if the truck ride doesn't kill 'em."

It would take a total of six attacks to clear the west bank of the Roer River. There were two other attacks taking place at the same time. Coming from Koslar in the middle, was L Company of the 116th. They were heading directly for the stadium. Company A was coming from the north and B Company was coming up from the south of the city of Julich. When the *Sportplatz* was finally taken, one hundred German troops were captured, along with ten machine guns, and several 88 mm self-propelled guns. Several artillery pieces were captured that were pre-registered, which meant they were fixed to fire at a specific point where the advancing American troops would be.

There were several other things that none of the attacking troops knew. These items of critical intelligence were crucial to the final clearing of the west side of the river on December 9th, 1944.

Unfortunately, these intelligence items were not available for the first attack made by L Company.

First, the blockhouse that the captain and L Company that had received withering machine gun fire from had originally been a dressing room for swimmers and soccer players. It had recently been reinforced, by the German defenders, with massive concrete beams. It took a concentrated air attack to destroy the fortification. Second, the gunfire that was so intense, coming from the tree line, was coming from an elaborate system of tunnels, bunkers, and catacombs. These were ancient stone and earthen fortifications built by the French, when the city was called *Juliers,* and later defenders. It was called a *Tete-de-pont* or Napoleonic bridgehead. It was constructed at the end of a bridge to prevent an enemy from crossing the river and entering the city. It was currently being utilized effectively by the retreating German Army. The fortifications defended the early Roman city of *Juliacum* against possible advancing forces from the west. The fortification in the trees commanded the high ground west of the river and was not easily seen or knocked out by air bombardment. The fortifications which stretched for over half a mile along the river were shaped like a three-pointed crown, with the points facing west.

The structure was low and surrounded by a moat. It was built along the west side of the river to protect the bridges over the river. Defending forces could cross the river and enter the back side of the crown and fire at advancing forces from inside the massive structure. Machine gun trenches also stretched along the base of the crown, parallel to the river to prevent any advances from the river. The above ground swimming pool stood to the north along the river; then came the tennis courts, next lay the athletic fields inside the earthen oval, and then stood the ancient fortifications.

It was an impressive and elaborate athletic complex. The point of the crown in the fortifications closest to the athletic field was the source of the machine gun fire because the reach of the bullets from the guns could easily cover one thousand yards to the west.

This is the reason why, when the captain saw the topographical map of the area, he had been puzzled why the Roer River ran through the high ground and not around it like a river naturally does. The high ground west of the river had been built up by thousands of years of defensive preparations by the successive defenders of the city. But these earthen alterations couldn't be seen from the air or ground because they were overgrown with trees, underbrush, and other vegetation.

Third, the swimming pool was above ground and heavily fortified. The lower level was surrounded on the west, south, and east sides by concrete dressing rooms that made excellent defensive positions. The east side was open and overlooked the river from a catwalk running north to south. The swimming pool served also as an observation point, because it overlooked the river bottoms to the west, and it had a diving tower which also provided an excellent elevated observation post.

Finally, and most important, the oval that the company had briefly captured was an athletic field surrounded by a very long bicycle racing track. The track was almost five hundred yards around and sloped from low to high with a brick wall on the top to keep racers from careening over the top. The track was dirt, and the defenders had dug into the inner part of the track on the slope.

There were no entrances, so the racer simply lifted a bicycle over the wall to begin circling the track. To American military observers and command officers, this race track was very confusing, because most Americans, at this time, had never seen a velodrome because cycling wasn't as popular in the United States as it was in Europe. Consequently, most of the American soldiers who fought for control of this structure didn't know what it was.

Air attacks also had difficulty reducing the 88 mm artillery guns in Julich. The German defenders had placed the 88s in the old citadel in the city. The citadel was a four-hundred-year-old fort with walls forty-four-feet thick. The citadel had an intricate tunnel system and a moat surrounding one hundred and fifty-foot-high walls. Along with the 88mm self-propelled guns, the 88mm artillery guns fired from their advantageous positions. Three months later, after massive air bombardment, the city fell in late February. The city was reduced to rubble. The citadel was never rebuilt, but the city, like most European cities, was rebuilt. Only the foundations of the fort remain.

Julich Sportpalast Hit by U.S. Planes

It just took 120 seconds to get quarter-ton bombs thudding into the enemy-held Julich Sportpalast after the 29th Division had requested fighter-bomber support, it was revealed today.

Three flights of the 29th TAC fighter-bombers were circling over Schophoven, waiting for the 30th Division radio to approve another target, when the 29th Division called the 29th Corps Air Support officer, Major D.R. McGovern of Providence, R. I.

Major McGovern was about to call for fresh air support when the 30th Division decided they didn't need the fighters. At a nod from McGovern, S. Sgt. Joseph A. Buckling Jr. of Staunton, Ill. radioed the fighters over Schophoven to fly north and attack the Sportplast. (*The Stars and Stripes,* Vol. 1, No. 138, Dec. 12, 1944)

During this time, the Battle of the Bulge, which had begun in December, was raging south of the area of the *Sportplatz.* The crates of 88 shells the captain had noticed lined up on the north to south railroad tracks were destined for the new German Army offensive. Unfortunately for the retreating German Army, the American Army had moved so quickly across Belgium and Holland, the German Army didn't have time to re-position them and most of the German railcars had been destroyed. The crates foretold the coming offensive but the American command apparently did not take notice or had more important problems to tackle.

His eyes opened and he saw the ceiling of a room that had tall glass windows. He closed them and was out for another two hours. When he did finally open his eyes, he couldn't speak. He had lost his voice. He tried several more times, but he still couldn't speak. He gave up and waited for a few more hours.

The next time he awoke he was delirious.

In his delirium, he kept repeating, "Gotta get to the clerk to get the day reports done." But, the day reports concerning the battle at the *Sportplatz* were never written. He would have been the officer to report the activities of the company, but he was not in a condition to complete the reports.

"Finally," he said, "Where?"

"Where am I?"

"I think the captain is coming around."

"Welcome back to war, captain. "

The slight hostility of their gallows humor was driven by the fact that the attitude of most enlisted men toward the officers ranged between passive indifference and outright hostility, but most knew to keep their traps shut in the presence of officers.

"We don't get many officers in here."

"Yea, we don't want to lose our highest ranking guest."

"Where am I?"

"You're in an aid station in Koslar."

His head was splitting and throbbing with pain, and he kept slipping in and out of consciousness, and he was only vaguely aware of his surroundings.

"My head"

"The morphine will take effect soon."

"God, I hope so."

After lying awake on the cot for a few minutes, he looked over at the private he recognized on the cot next to him. The private looked worse than anyone could imagine.

He was covered in mud from head to foot and bandaged in several places. His eyes had a hollow look and the bones of his face made him look like his head was a skin covered skull.

"Hi, captain."

"How are you doing private?" It was Private McCracken. Somehow his comrades had helped get him back to safety. They had drug, carried, and wheeled him all the way from the racetrack to the aid station.

My God, these kids are really tough, and he's damn lucky!

"Don't worry about me. I'm just a little knicked-up.....thank God we got out of there, captain."

He looked at the captain and they looked at each other, each knowing from what they had escaped. It looked like his bandages covered most of his body, and the blood was showing on the bandage just below his knee.

"We're getting out of here soon private."

"On a truck in the morning," the medic said.

The medic added, "Back to Herleen, and I don't know where after that. There'll be more coming in here anytime, so we gotta get you out to make room for new men coming in."

He looked around the aid station and the wounded soldiers were eating hot oatmeal with their hands. Oatmeal was considered a real treat, but eating with their hands and fingers looked odd and primitive. Their mess kits had been discarded long ago. They weren't needed in a fight, added extra weight, and the utensils in the kits made too much noise rattling around in their packs.

He felt for the pockets in his field jacket to see if he still had his pipe and tobacco. They were still in the pockets. When none of the medics were around, he felt for his billfold. It was still in his pocket. He took out the pictures of Skip, unfolded them, looked at them again, and wept tears of joy. After being wounded in France, spending months in the hospitals in England, and surviving the attack on the *Sportplatz*, he was going home to see her.

He paused for a few minutes, collected his emotions, returned to his present situation, and thought, *Damn, I used to sell oatmeal before Pearl Harbor and now it is as welcome as Texas steak.*

The other thing that he immediately noticed about the aid station was that it was heated. It was a glorious heat that he guessed was coming from a kerosene heater, or steam heat in the building. He didn't care where it was coming from. He hadn't felt any heat in a week since leaving Herleen, only cold and wetness. The next thing he noticed and felt was that he was wearing dry socks. It felt gloriously good to get some dry socks and dry boots. He had to dry the boots before he could put them back on. The warmth of the building made him notice that it was still drizzling outside as he looked through the glass windows of the old building. What he didn't know, was that the current winter was the coldest on record in the Rhineland Plain in fifty years.

"Okay, listen up you dogfaces. You're all leaving in the morning on trucks to Herleen."

We don't have any clean uniforms at this five-star hotel, but back at the hospital, they'll get you all cleaned up."

He looked around and could immediately see some of the men with major wounds were gonna have a tough time on the bouncing trucks when their wounds got disturbed. All of them had been given sulfa drugs to curb infections and clear up the GIs. He thought about another truck ride to a hospital. He had done that before and it was going to be a rough trip.

His clothes were drying out and getting stiff. The mud was starting to break off in little pieces at the knees and elbows. He knew he didn't look like a captain and didn't think he could go back into the lines. But, he agonized about what happened to the company and the men.

He wondered, *Who brought me in? How long have I been out?   How many men survived the last 88 barrage?*

"Medic! Who brought the two of us in?"

"I dunno. You were here when the two of us came up from Englesdorf. You were unconscious when I got here."

He couldn't remember much about anything that happened before he woke up in the aid station. He knew he was still weak from exhaustion, disoriented, and in pain.

What the hell, he thought I'll probably never know what happened.

The company clerk's entries were:

Shearer, Robert L. capt Hq 3 bn 5 Dec 44 fr dy to hospital NBC

Shearer, Robert L. capt Hq Co 3 bn 7 Dec 44 dropped for rations from Dec 5
Shearer, Robert L. capt Hq 3 bn 8 Dec 44 fr hosp NBC to dropped from rolls.

The deuce-and-a-half left at 7:00 a.m. for Herleen, passing thousands of soldiers and vehicles headed for the front and the continuing battle for Julich. The mud was deep, the roads were deeply rutted from all the traffic, and the trip was bumpy. The truck lurched from side to side and then heaved forward when the huge, cleated tires dug their way out of each mud hole. Bandaged soldiers were jostled and bounced around, blood dripping from the bandages. Many were crying and moaning. But, they were going home with "million dollar wounds." The trucks were carrying the living casualties of the war away from the death and destruction. Many others did not make the trip alive. Some died in route.

In Herleen, he got clean clothes and took a bath, the first in weeks. He noticed his clothes were so stiff he could stand them up against a wall. After he had returned home to Iowa, a package arrived in the mail from a doctor in Illinois whom he had met in Herleen. In the package, he found his combat long wool overcoat and his pistol holster.

The overcoat had been cleaned and the holster was empty. He knew it was his holster because he always discarded the military issue holster with a covering flap because it took too long to get to the pistol. In place of the issue holster, he preferred an open holster with a strap that snapped over the hammer. This particular holster had a basket weave design, so it was unmistakable. Why the package was sent and where it was mailed from, remains a puzzle. His best guess was that it was mailed to him by the doctor he met in the hospital in Liege. He wasn't in Herleen long before he was on another truck to Liege, Belgium, and the battalion hospital.

After a brief stay at the hospital, he was loaded on a forty-and-eight again headed for Brussels, Belgium. On the trip to Brussels, he noticed an unusual but familiar sight. Looking through the open slats of the cattle car, he could see the tracks were lined with crates of food that were spoiling, based on the terrible smell. Many of the crates were marked: U.S. BEEF. The boxcars heading for the front had been hastily emptied to accommodate retreating American troops when the Battle of the Bulge had begun.

In Herleen, Liege, and all cities along the way, there were thousands of slave laborers, mostly Polish women fleeing in all directions. The women had been forced into prostitution or slave labor in German factories and on German farms. Now with their masters gone, they were dispersing in all directions in complete chaos. The angry women frequently tried to obtain weapons from American troops to go back and shoot their slave masters. They clogged the roads and cities and made a mess of military traffic and communications.

He was checked into the hospital in Brussels sometime late in December. He hadn't been there long when the hospital orderlies came running down the wards and told the patients who could walk to leave immediately. They walked to the railroad tracks heading for Paris. They were marched down the tracks by the hospital orderlies. The orderlies said the Germans were still counterattacking and no rail cars or trucks were available because they were being used to move retreating American troops. So everything, both troops and supplies, had to shift into reverse and go the other direction. He figured that was why all of the food had been unloaded on the way to Brussels. It also became clear that was the reason why the 88 crates in Koslar were lined up going south. The German Army had been planning a major winter offensive.

The patients who had been in the process of being treated for anxiety and depression were passing out on the tracks. The orderlies went up and down the line of men putting sugar water on their tongues to offset the effects of insulin shock therapy.

Insulin shock therapy was invented in 1939, and at the time, was the most popular new treatment for depression other than electroconvulsive therapy (ECT). He had been scheduled for insulin to treat his depression but was rushed onto the tracks before he could be treated. Most of the patients who were injured and disoriented were suffering from severe depression or anxiety.

Eventually, the patients got back on freight cars and made it to Paris. Paris was completely overcrowded and gridlocked. All of the roads leading in and out of the city were jammed with soldiers and vehicles. Most men and vehicles were trying to get to the front lines, and some were going the other direction. From the railroad yards, the wounded soldiers were supposed to go to a hospital in the central part of the city. It took hours for the truck to get to its destination.

The hospital in Paris was a converted orphanage. It had small beds, little tables, and chairs, as well as small urinals in the bathroom. It was full of wounded soldiers and soldiers who were deemed to have combat fatigue or shell shock.

From Paris, he traveled on a boat across the English Channel. He passed the Isle of Wight on January 1st, 1945 and on to the port of Southampton, England. The trip from Southampton to the United States took three weeks aboard the hospital ship, Cristobal. The trip was uneventful except for the orderlies running up and down the decks at night trying to keep wounded and depressed soldiers from jumping overboard into the ocean. Some of the desperate men were successful.

He went to Kennedy General Hospital in Memphis, Tennessee. He wrote the following letter:

> Wd B 7
> Kennedy General Hospital
> Memphis, Tennessee
> May 1, 1945

Dear Skip:

Hi, Toots. I bought something for you that will really make a flapper out of you. Something that will give you that old wolf call every time you pass the wolves. I'll give it to you when you come down.

Col. Bender was shot by his own men in France. Col. Martin was killed by a mine. Played tennis all morning. When you come down be sure to bring your summer clothes and tennis shoes and outfit. We'll play here as the courts are very nice.

Tomorrow nite the cadet nurses are inviting all of the patient officers to a wiener roast. Doc and I and all the half wits here are going.

What do you think about bringing Bobby along down or would it be too much trouble. Maybe it would be too much trouble as he'd have to eat regularly.

> Bye sweet
> All my love
> Bob

After six months as a patient at Kennedy General Hospital, he was transferred to Brook General Hospital in San Antonio, Texas where he had a disability hearing. The following is a transcript of that hearing:

Member of the board: Do you wish to be retired from active service in the army of the United States?

Capt. Shearer: Yes.

Member of the board: State the nature of your disability, its causes and how long you have suffered from it   Capt. Shearer: I guess it's psychoneurosis. That's what the doctors say.

Recorder: Tell the Board in you own terms why you can't do duty.

Capt. Shearer: Well, I just can't seem to stand the pressure. I go to pieces very easily and lose my temper and I can't sleep. I get "crying jags" at the slightest show of sentiment, either at a church or theater or seeing wounded soldiers or – well, I guess that's all.

Member of the Board: What was your profession in civilian life?

Capt. Shearer: I was a salesman.

Member of the Board: What did you sell?

Capt. Shearer: Rolled oats.

Member of the Board: Did you travel on the road?

Capt. Shearer: Yes, sir.

Member of the Board: How long has it been since you came out of the front lines?

Capt. Shearer: Since December 5, 1944.

Member of the Board: Have you been this way ever since?

Capt. Shearer: Yes, sir.

Member of the Board: Have you had no improvement?

Capt. Shearer: Yes, sir, there has been a lot of improvement. I was in pretty bad shape when I came out. I could hardly talk, my hands were paralyzed, and I was pretty exhausted.

Recorder: Are there any further questions by the Board?

Member of the Board: Have you always been nervous? Were you nervous in childhood?

Capt. Shearer: Well, I would say to some extent, but I used to – when a thing went wrong, I could buckle down and I could handle situations, but I can't do that now anymore.

Member of the Board: Did you lose your temper easily?

Capt. Shearer: No, sir – you mean before?

Member of the Board: I notice in your history, you say you cannot sleep at night. How much do you sleep in the daytime?

Capt. Shearer: Well, on the ward, I usually rest a little bit after lunch, but other than that, I don't sleep much during the daytime. At night, I cannot sleep because – if I start thinking about fighting, I can't get to sleep, and if I do get to sleep, I start jerking and sometimes sit straight up and it is too bad.

Member of the board: Do you believe you could go back and perform duty on a limited duty status and be given the opportunity to recover from this trouble?

Capt. Shearer: Well, the doctors say they have done all they can do for me.

Member of the Board: The doctors say they have done all they can do for you, so what improvements are to be made from now on, you will have to accomplish yourself.

Capt. Shearer: I don't believe I could do limited duty. I would hate to risk any job that might put me back in the hospital. People irritate me terribly. I don't go downtown very often, I don't listen to the radio, as noise irritates me.

Member of the Board: Would a little self-discipline help – a little tolerance?

Capt. Shearer: Well, I have tried that with my family, but I still "fly off the handle" and it is kind of a source of worry to me there.

Member of the Board: Where is your home?

Capt. Shearer: Toledo, Iowa.

Member of the Board: How much schooling have you had?

Capt. Shearer: I have a B.A. degree.

Member of the Board: How successful were you in civilian life?

Capt. Shearer: Well, I had a good income. I owned my own car, and would say I was fairly successful.

Member of the Board: How much money did you make?

Capt. Shearer: About $240.00 a month and expenses.

Member of the Board: Did you own your home?

Capt. Shearer: I do now, sir.

Member of the Board: How much of a family have you?

Capt. Shearer: A wife, two children, and a sister to take care of.

Member of the Board: How old are you?

Capt. Shearer: Thirty-two, sir.

Member of the Board: What was the source of your commission?

Capt. Shearer: ROTC.

Member of the Board: When did you come on active duty?

Capt. Shearer: March 4, 1942.

Member of the Board: What unit were you with in combat?

Capt. Shearer: 29th Division, 116th Infantry.

Member of the Board: How long had you been with that Regiment?

Capt. Shearer: Since D plus 5.

Member of the Board: Where were you before that?

Capt. Shearer: I was with the 95th Division, and then the 97th Division, and then I went overseas as a replacement.

Member of the Board: What were your duties in the 97th Division?

Capt. Shearer: Company Commander of a heavy weapons company.

Member of the Board: What were your duties in the 95th Division?

Capt. Shearer: I was Company Commander of a rifle company.

Member of the Board: When were you transferred from the 95th to the 97th?

Capt. Shearer: Right after basic training. A 95th cadre went to the 97th.

Member of the Board: On what date?

Capt. Shearer: Shortly after New Years of 1943.

Member of the Board: Were you a Captain at that time?
Capt. Shearer: No, sir.

Member of the Board: You were a Company Commander in the 5th, were you not?

Capt. Shearer: Yes, sir. I was a First Lieutenant, sir.

Member of the Board: How long had you been a First Lieutenant?

Capt. Shearer: Since I came on active duty.

Member of the Board: You came on active duty as a First Lieutenant?

Capt. Shearer: Yes, sir. I was a First Lieutenant for nine months.

Member of the Board: What was the reason for your transfer from the 97th Division?

Capt. Shearer: Well, they took everybody – the Commanding General, the Colonel commanding the Regiment; they took everybody who was physically fit.

Member of the Board: From the 97th, did you go overseas as casuals?

Capt. Shearer: Yes, sir.

Member of the Board: When were you promoted to Captain?

Capt. Shearer: 5 October 1943.

Member of the Board: This was after you joined the 97th then?

Capt. Shearer: Yes, sir.
Recorder: Are there any further questions, gentlemen?

Member of the Board: Where do you intend to settle down after the war?

Capt. Shearer: I think I will go back to Toledo and probably work on the farm for a little while.

Member of the Board: Is that where you own your home?

Capt. Shearer: Yes, sir.

Recorder: Captain, have you any further evidence to present to the Board at this time?

Capt. Shearer: No, sir.

Recorder: State whether or not this officer is incapacitated for active service.

Capt. Shelton: In our opinion, he is.

Recorder: State the cause or causes of such incapacity.

Capt. Shelton: Anxiety state, severe, chronic; external stress, mild; 30 days of front line combat; predisposition, moderate; estimated impairment, marked.

Recorder: State the date on which such incapacity originated.

Capt. Shelton: It originated the latter part of June 1944.

Recorder: State whether or not such incapacity is incident to the Service.

Capt. Shelton: Yes, sir.

Recorder: State whether or not such incapacity is permanent.

Capt. Shelton: Yes, sir.

Recorder: State whether or not this officer is physically qualified to perform Limited Service.

Capt. Shelton: No, sir.

Member of the Board: Can this officer be entrusted on his own custody?

Capt. Shelton: Yes, sir.

Recorder: Captain Morales, do you concur in Captain Shelton's testimony?

Capt. Morales: Yes, sir.

Recorder: Captain Shearer, do you have any questions to as the medical witnesses?

Capt. Shearer: No, sir.

Recorder: Are there any questions by the Board?

Member of the Board: Would further treatment be of any benefit to this officer?

Capt. Shelton: No, sir. I feel that further hospitalization – active hospitalization – would probably tend to fix this particular condition. He needs treatment, yes, sir, but he needs it under a different environment than we can give him here. I feel that back on the farm, where the responsibilities and traumas associated with Army life are at a minimum, he will have his best opportunity to improve.

Member of the Board: Would it be of any benefit to this officer to send him on Limited Service, where he would have the opportunity to receive treatment?

Capt. Shelton: He is incapable of any type of service, Colonel.

Member of the Board: How much predisposition existed in this case?

Capt. Shelton: Moderate, sir.

Member of the Board: Captain Shelton, you say this originated in June 1944. Is that the time he had his flesh wound in the hip?

Capt. Shelton: No, sir, I think he had his flesh wound on the tenth or twelfth of July. That is an estimate on my part, Colonel. I would say that, following hospitalization for his wound, it was noticed that he showed a considerable degree of anxiety, and that usually is an incipient phase, so I just assumed that the latter part of the month was when it began to develop. I should say that the thirty days – approximately thirty days – of frontline combat does not include a month or more in the active combat zone. For example, he was in a Replacement Depot that was under constant bombing and artillery for several weeks before and then when he went back up to the front lines, I believe he also had some administrative job a short time. I am including in the thirty days the actual front line combat as a company commander. Actually, he was under combat conditions about two and a half times that much.

Recorder: Are there any further questions, gentlemen? There were none, and the medical witnesses, Captain Shelton and Captain Morales were excused and left the room.

Recorder: Captain Shearer, have you any further testimony to offer, or would you like to make a statement under oath or not under oath.

Capt. Shearer: About the last time I was up, we were cut off for three days and three nights – myself and my thirty men – and the Germans used flame throwers on us, self-propelled guns, and artillery fire, and finally we were ordered to withdraw and I got all of my men out, I just couldn't stand the let-down, I guess. That is the story. I had one breakdown in the hospital in England after I was hit, and it took me six weeks to get over that, and it took me nine months to get over the second one, and I hate to risk the third one. That is all, I guess.

Member of the Board: Do you feel that is a normal reaction to this circumstance?

Capt. Shearer: Well, I guess it is. I have a lot of my men – not a lot, but a few – who reacted that way, and one officer who was there all the way from Normandy to the Rhur River, and he finally had to be pulled out.

Recorder: I have no further evidence to introduce.

President of the Board: If there is not further evidence to be introduced, the Board will be closed.

The board was closed for deliberation and after mature consideration, finds that Captain Robert L. Shearer, 0361206, Infantry, Army of the United States, (ORC), is incapacitated for active service; that said incapacity is the result of an incident of service; that the cause of said incapacity is: Anxiety state, severe, chronic; external stress, mild, 30 days of front line combat, predisposition, moderate; estimated impairment, marked; that the cause of said incapacity is not an incident of service; that said incapacity was first manifested in or about June 1944; and that said incapacity is permanent.

The Board was opened and the President announces the Board's findings to Captain Shearer.

The President of the Board made the following statement in open session:

> President of the Board: The Board further recommends that you be examined at a fixed Army installation at intervals of not less than six months for purposes of re-evaluation of your case to determine your physical conditions existing at that time

Years later, the officer advised of his right to file an application for pension.

Years later, the captain was walking into a Walmart store in Texas when he saw a man, in the store's entrance, who had a cap with a blue and gray 29th Division patch on it. The older gentleman was talking to another older gentleman who was a greeter for the store. Seeing the familiar patch, he decided to find out a bit more about the man. He went up to the man with a patch on his cap and got his attention.

"Hello…Were you in the 29th?"

"Yes sir, I was."

"What outfit?"

"A Company of the 115th."

"In the Rhineland?"

"Yea."

"Where?"

"On the Roer. At Julich. Well, actually west of the city."

"Really. I made the first attack on the *Sportplatz* about the 3rd of December, 1944."

"Damn! I was in the last attack on the 9th at the swimming pool."

"I was a private. What were you?"

"A captain, L Company commander in the 116th.

"Whatta you doing now?"

"I'm a retired dentist. Went to dental school after the war.

How about you?"

"I'm retired too…food broker business."

"Did you hear about what we found in the swimming pool?"

"No, I never got that far. Haven't heard a thing."

"We found sixteen dead American 29ers at the bottom of the dry swimming pool. All had been stripped and strangled with bathrobe cords from the dressing rooms. They had surrendered in one of the earlier attacks."

He felt himself getting lightheaded and emotional. Tears began to well up.

"Yeah. The Germans were trying to take prisoners for their uniforms---you know, no bullet or shrapnel holes in them for the upcoming Battle of the Bulge down south of Julich. They wanted them so that they could impersonate American troops and disrupt the American counterattack. Poor bastards."

If You're Captured, Button Your Lip—Stick to a Polite Dead-Pan Act

Of all the words in any language, there is one phrase that intelligence officers dread to hear from a prisoner who is brought in for questioning. In German, it is *'Es tut mir lied.'* In Italian, it is *'Molte scuse.'* In American it is simply 'I'm sorry.' It is the perfect answer for any and all questions an enemy questioner may ask, according to U. S. officers who have lately interviewed a great many prisoners.

Back in training, our men saw a British orientation film entitled, 'Name, Rank, and Serial Number,' which explained what to do and say if you happened to be captured.

But there are any number of ways to circumvent the rules if the questioner is a good psychologist, out officers say.

Here are a few warning hints, from men who question prisoners at the front line, on how to act if captured:

Always be polite and military. This attitude is the strongest weapon for disarming the enemy questioner. If you are taken before someone who outranks you, salute even if it makes you squirm. Stand at attention until told to relax. And don't open your mouth until you are compelled to by common courtesy, then give a polite answer that says nothing.

It's best to call the enemy questioner 'Sir' or name his rank if you can figure out what it is. Then when you answer 'I'm sorry sir' to his questions, there isn't much he can do about it.

A German trick employed to break down that 'I'm sorry, sir' is this question: 'Do you think you Americans can beat us Germans?' Any number of Yanks answer, 'You're damned right we can,' whereupon the German asks, 'Why?' You can't very well answer that one without some proof, so you tell a few things the enemy wants to know. If you fall for that trick, the best way to answer the 'Why?' question is to come back fast with the stock reply, 'I'm sorry, sir.'

If the constant repetition of that phrase makes you feel like a parrot or a dummy, don't let it get you down; the investigator is just as frustrated as you are. If you vary your answer by saying, 'I can't answer that,' the questioner will whip back swiftly with the words, 'You mean you can't or you won't?' and then you're in a hole again.

The Germans like to hint they'll do all sorts of things to you if you persist in saying nothing, but they won't do anything for fear we will do the same to their prisoners.

Don't try to show off if you are captured, our officers advise because the men who question you are among the brainiest in the enemy army. Sometimes the college man struts his learning and lets on he's above the common run of prisoners in intelligence, which just about makes him the dumbest prisoner there is. The investigator gets that kind of soldier talking about what he did in civilian life, one question leads to another and, once you start talking, you can't stop because you can't very well refuse to answer a question after you've already answered a dozen others.

Finally, if you happen to capture prisoners yourself, don't take any souvenirs before turning the soldiers in. Investigators can learn a hell of a lot from letters and personal effects. They use them to find out who the prisoner is, and once in possession of that fact, they can often start the long chain of questions that make the prisoner talk.

(Corporal John M Willig, *Yank, The Army Weekly,* August 22nd, 1943)

Fortunately for him and his men, he hadn't surrendered at the *Sportplatz.* Unfortunately, he and many of his men became casualties at the complex of athletic facilities.

The Rhineland campaign, in November and December of 1944, had cost the 29th Division some twenty-six hundred battle casualties, of whom five hundred were killed in action or died of wounds. Eleven hundred soldiers were wounded. Steady rains, cold temperatures, and plummeting morale had also triggered more than one thousand non-battle casualties, mostly trench foot, and combat exhaustion cases. (Balkoski, J., *Our Tortured Souls,* Stackpole Books, 2013, p.330)

For him, the attack on the *Sportplatz* was *fini la guere* or the end of the war.

Acknowledgements

The following sources are acknowledged as providing valuable contribution to the construction of this account:

Balkoski, Joseph., *Our Tortured Souls,* (2013), Stackpole Books, Mechanicsburg, PA.

Cawthon, Charles R. "July, 1944: St. So," *American Heritage,* June 1974, Vol.XXV, No. 4, 4-11.

Donceel, Don, 29th Division, personal communication.

Ewing, Joseph H., "29 Let's Go!" *Infantry Journal Press,* Washington, D.C.

Harris, Fletcher, Lieutenant, Co. B, 1st Br., 115th Inf. Regt. 29th division, Personal communication.

Historical Division, War Department "St. Lo"

McIntosh, Edwin A., *"Heaven, Hell, or Home, "*29th Division, Unpublished manuscript and personal communication.

The 29th Infantry Division Morning Reports, World War Two, http:// www.29idmorningrpt.com/